CRIME FILES:
FOUR-MINUTE FORENSIC MYSTERIES

Body of Evidence

CRIME FILES:

FOUR-MINUTE FORENSIC MYSTERIES

Body of Evidence

By Jeremy Brown

Scholastic Inc.

New York   Toronto   London   Sydney
Mexico City   New Delhi   Hong Kong   Buenos Aires

ISBN 0-439-76934-5

Design by Steve Scott

12 11 10 9 8 7 6 5 4   8 9 10 11/0
Printed in the U.S.A.
First printing, March 2006

For my parents, Roger and Melissa, who showed me that sometimes all you need is a good book and a warm place to read it. Without their support, I might be a completely different person. But they would still be proud.

Table of Contents

CRIME FILES:
FOUR-MINUTE FORENSIC MYSTERIES

Body of Evidence

PERSONNEL FILE

CSI Wes Burton: Burton is a witty, intelligent investigator who loves the problem-solving nature of crime scene investigation. His signature fly fisherman's vest, bristling with evidence-gathering tools, is a welcome sight at any crime scene (except those run by Detective Gibson). Not much surprises Burton, including a criminal's ability to weave a nearly perfect lie. He usually prefers evidence analysis to talking with witnesses and suspects because, unlike people, "evidence stands up; it does not lie." He appreciates Detective Radley's interviewing skills and her interest in *why* a crime occurred, because it allows him to focus on the *how*.

Detective Erin Radley: At six-foot-one, Detective Radley can be an intimidating woman. Her motto, "Convict them with kindness," seems in conflict with her physical appearance, but it is that contradiction that keeps suspects off balance and talking to her. When a woman of her stature hands you a blanket and hot chocolate, then asks why you stabbed your wife, it's hard to concentrate on your lie. Radley has a master's degree in psychology and tends to focus on the *why* of a case. She plans to publish a study someday on what compels criminals to commit their crimes. Working with Burton presents plenty of odd situations that will help her book stand out. She appreciates Burton's dedication to solving crimes and his ability to lighten situations that most individuals would find disturbing and depressing.

Detective Frank Gibson: Gibson is what he would call "old school," using intimidation and a loud voice to get a confession rather than patience and by-the-book techniques. In some cases his approach is required, such as when a kidnapper won't divulge the location of his latest victim, but for the most part Burton and his team do not appreciate Gibson's presence at a crime scene. Gibson and Burton constantly clash with each other, and when it comes to solving a crime, they have an unspoken competition to see who can identify the perpetrator first. The perps don't stand a chance.

Mike Trellis: Trellis is Burton's CSI technician assistant. He specializes in trace analysis, arson, and horrible jokes, such as commenting that a shooting victim died from "Too much lead in his diet." It doesn't help that he follows every joke with "Get it?" Burton knows that when Trellis is working on a case, he can expect close attention to detail, exhaustive analysis of evidence, and dedication to finding the guilty party. Detective Gibson likes to pick on Trellis, but the young technician has a knack for frustrating the burly cop, and for that, Burton likes him even more.

Lauren Crown: Dr. Crown is a shy, almost reclusive forensic pathologist. A genius in her field, she is nearly incapable of having a normal conversation. However, she is quick to recite the qualifications of a forensic pathologist[1] should anyone refer to her as a medical examiner, or worse, a coroner. She can determine a corpse's time of death within ten minutes just by looking at it, but she has no idea who the president of the United States is — and doesn't care.

Ed: Ed, short for Exhibit D, is a search-and-rescue border collie. She was adopted and trained by Burton after being admitted as evidence in a case against her owner, a methamphetamine dealer. Her fur contained trace elements of the ingredients used to make crystal meth, and the dealer was convicted. She can follow ground and air scent and is in training to become a certified cadaver dog as well.

Burian U. Gorlach: Burian, or Bug, as he prefers to be called, is a Russian immigrant and the owner of Sensitive Cleaners, a company that cleans and decontaminates crime scenes when an investigation is complete. Bug is anything but sensitive, muttering in semi-English and cackling while he rips up bloodstained carpets and vacuums biohazards.

---

[1] As a physician who specializes in the investigation of sudden, unexpected, and violent deaths, the forensic pathologist attempts to determine the identification of the deceased, the time of death, the manner of death (natural, accident, suicide, or homicide), the cause of death, if the death was by injury, and the nature of the instrument used to cause the death, using methods such as toxicology, firearms examination (wound ballistics), trace evidence, forensic serology, and DNA technology.

The Defense Rests in Peace

CSI Wes Burton walked into the lawyer's office and immediately bristled. It wasn't seeing a corpse that disturbed him; it was the fact that he *didn't* see one. The dozen or so breathing people in the room were obstructing his view.

"Which one of you is dead?" he asked. A stunned silence followed as the officers, EMTs, and a short, shaken woman looked at him. "If it isn't you, there's no reason for you to be at this crime scene," said Burton. Detective Erin Radley, who was used to his behavior, tried to hide a smile.

As everyone filed out of the office, Burton took his custom-made CRIME SCENE — DO NOT CROSS / CRIME SEEN? STICK AROUND yellow tape out of pocket 2 of the fly fisherman's vest he wore to every crime scene. The thirty or so other pockets on the vest bulged and rattled with everything from latex gloves to a handheld ultraviolet light. He rarely came across a situation that required something that wasn't in those pockets. Radley stayed where she was, as far from the body as possible, to avoid further contaminating the scene. She had on her usual black leather jacket, and its mid-thigh length made her look even taller than usual.

One of the emergency medical technicians helped the distressed woman through the doorway. "We'll check your heart rate right away, Miss Porter. I'm sure it's nothing serious." To

Burton, he said, "She has some heart-attack symptoms. If they continue, we'll have to take her to the ER."

Burton nodded. "Just keep all of her clothes, and don't let her shower." He stretched the yellow tape across the doorway and secured it. To him, that thin piece of plastic represented a brick wall with armed sentries on top. Maybe even a helicopter or two.

"What do we have, Detective Radley?" Burton asked as he made his way to the other side of the room, careful not to disturb anything. The two client chairs in front of the desk seemed in place, bua problem for Brent Cordova, former attorney-at-law, who was faceup on the floor behind his enormous desk.

"Dead lawyer," she said, opening her notepad. "Only a few million suspects."

"Shotgun to the chest?" Burton asked.

"Looks like it," Radley said. "The legal assistant, Miss Porter, says that Cordova had been planning on closing his practice and retiring next month, and he was handing off all his defense cases on a first-come, first-served basis. She says the clients weren't happy and have been calling with nasty messages."

"He didn't know making murder suspects mad can have bad side effects?" Burton asked. "Like getting murdered?"

"You'd think he would," Radley said. "Only three of his current clients are on trial for murder, and they're being

tracked down right now. We'll see how their alibis look."
Radley thought for a moment, then went on. "If one of them did it, I hope he'll talk to me about why."

"Are you still writing that book of yours?" Burton asked.

"Yes," she said. "I've got some fascinating stuff so far." Radley, who had a master's degree in psychology, had been compiling case studies for years that focused on why criminals committed their crimes. She planned to publish them for the law enforcement community.

"I still don't get it," Burton said. "The *why* doesn't prove anything. You can't convict anyone on a reason or motive; you have to know *how* they did it."

"True," Radley said. "But if we find out why a murder took place, maybe we can prevent the next one from happening at all."

"But people can lie about why they did something," Burton said, "and you might not be able to prove that they're lying. Evidence stands up in court. It does not lie."

"So you're always telling me," said Radley.

Burton took a closer look at the entrance wound on the body. It was on Cordova's upper left chest, with gunshot residue and small burns on his skin and the tatters of his shirt. There was no visible exit of pellets or slugs, but from the pattern and depth of the wound, he could see that the shot had entered at a 10-degree angle from Cordova's left side, at about the height of his shoulder.

Burton also saw that Cordova's chair, a high-backed leather throne, had gunshot residue on the upper left wing. "How tall are those three murder suspects?"

Radley pulled three folders from under her arm and checked through them. "Miss Porter pulled these for me. She's pretty upset. She passed the bar exam a month ago and has helped with some of these cases. She thinks if the killer comes back, she'll be next."

"Did she witness anything?" Burton asked.

"No, she says she found him like this, called us right away. Okay, here's the last one. The suspects are six-foot-three, five-foot-ten, and six feet even. Is that helpful?"

"Not to the shooter's case," Burton said.

The EMT stuck his head in over the crime scene tape. "Miss Porter's having some real trouble out here. Heart's racing like a jackrabbit. We're going to take her to the hospital for observation."

"That's fine," Burton said. "But let Detective Radley read her her rights first."

How did he know?

Burton's File

The entrance wound indicated that the fatal shot was close range (GSR and burns) and came from Cordova's left. He was seated and looking straight ahead when he was shot (GSR on chair, wound on left of face rather than front), indicating that

8

he trusted the shooter next to him. Two chairs in front of the large desk suggest all client contact is across the desk. The entrance wound angled slightly downward, indicating that the shooter was short. A tall shooter aiming at a sitting Cordova would have produced an entrance angle near 45 degrees.

Porter recently passed the bar exam, making her eligible to take over the practice, yet she was being passed over by Cordova. At the crime scene, the EMTs thought she had heart-attack symptoms: numbness or pain spreading to the shoulders, neck, or arms; anxiety; nervousness; cold, sweaty skin; increased or irregular heart rate — also symptoms of recently firing a shotgun into your boss's chest.

The Burning Question

Burton walked into the restaurant's kitchen; its stainless steel and tile surfaces were covered in soggy soot and burnt debris. The sprinklers had been shut off over an hour ago, but the overhead fixtures still dripped steadily. He brought head chef Nathan Olivo in with him, careful to keep the distraught man away from any evidence.

"I hope you like your steak well done," said Mike Trellis, Burton's CSI technician. He specialized in arson investigation and bad jokes. Burton laughed, the chef did not.

Trellis was using a fuel sniffer, which looked like a small cane attached to a lunch box, to check areas of the kitchen for traces of accelerant. Gasoline and kerosene were the most common, but he had seen arsonists use everything from Silly String to hair spray to start a fire.

"Can you tell me what happened here?" Burton asked.

"It was about a half hour after we closed. We were all in the bar toasting the end of the night when the kitchen just blew up. I started the toast tradition a few weeks ago when we got a mediocre review in the local restaurant guide. The toast is supposed to build morale and create team atmosphere — everyone was pretty down after that review. But the bad food wasn't our fault, it was the stove."

"The stove?" Burton said. "Was there a problem with it?"

"Problem? It was a piece of garbage," Olivo said. "Always burning entrées, scalding sauces, and stinking of gas; the

10

pilot light for one of the burners kept going out. I asked the manufacturers to replace it several times, but they refused, saying it was fine."

Trellis walked over to the blackened stove, the sniffer leading the way.

"Thank you, Mr. Olivo," Burton said, leading him toward the door. "Please step outside with the other employees and we'll finish up in here."

Burton shined his flashlight around the kitchen. "The room looks like there was a sudden explosion rather than a slow burn," he said. "And soot is covering just about every surface in here — walls, counters, and especially the ceiling and ceiling fans — so whatever happened, it sent residue everywhere. But what burned in order to make the soot? Soot results from imperfect burning, and natural gas burns cleanly, with no residue. I can't believe the kitchen had enough dust to cause this mess." Burton looked again at the ceiling and the black film covering it. "Wait a minute. Were the ceiling fans on when the kitchen blew?"

Trellis checked his notes. "The fan switch was in the on position, but the explosion knocked out the electricity, so they weren't spinning for long. The big exhaust ducts up there were off for the night."

"Let's try to get a fingerprint off of that fan switch," Burton said. He climbed onto the stainless steel island in the middle of the kitchen and took a closer look at one of the ceiling fans. It was caked with black soot, as was the ceiling above it. He reached above the fan and ran his finger along the top side of one of the blades. It came back with a white substance on it. Burton smelled it once, then touched it to his tongue.

"Mmm. Tastes like arson," he said.

How did he know?

Burton's File

Olivo's claim that the faulty stove caused the explosion could not have been true. The amount of soot in the room indicated an accelerant other than the natural gas from the stove, and the amount of residue on the ceiling and ceiling fans showed that a large amount of the accelerant was near the top of the room; the fans would have blown natural gas away from the ceiling.

The staff was out of the kitchen for thirty minutes when the explosion occurred; a leaking pilot light would require much more time to fill the kitchen with enough gas to cause the explosion.

Olivo wanted to blame his restaurant's poor review on the defective stove; instead he proved how good he was at burning things. He waited until his staff was safe in the bar, then turned on the ceiling fans, on which he had piled an accelerant that can easily be found in any kitchen: baking flour. In dust form, flour and other grains are explosive, something a chef would have known. Once the dust drifted down to the pilot lights, it was kitchen flambé.

No Day at the Beach

Burton read the printout from the gas chromatograph/mass spectrometer and nodded. The two samples he had submitted to the machine for analysis were from the steering wheel and driver's seat of Charlotte Haney's car. What was left of it, anyway. A 250-foot fall into a ravine full of boulders tends to do more than scuff the bumper.

As he expected, the samples were identical, with high amounts of zinc oxide and titanium dioxide. Burton made his way back to the interview room and entered to find Detective Frank Gibson questioning Ted Haney, Charlotte's husband and the only witness to the accident. Gibson was a bully and had a reputation for getting confessions before the crime lab could even sweep the scene. He claimed it saved him paperwork. Burton didn't particularly like his methods, but he saw their usefulness in some situations. Burton had a bit of a reputation himself; something to do with not liking bullies and lazy detectives.

"I already told you," Ted sputtered, "She got into the car to get the camera, and it started rolling. She was leaning in through the door of the backseat, so she couldn't tell the car was moving, and —"

"At what point did you start to push the car?" Detective Gibson interrupted. "Or did you just knock her unconscious and take your time rolling it over the cliff?"

"Hold on there, Detective," Burton said. "Mr. Haney is

a witness, not a suspect. If he becomes a suspect, we have to bring in the really bright light and crank the thermostat up to 110 degrees. You know that. Look at him, he's already sweating."

"What's your problem, Burton? Did you run out of pink outline chalk or something?" Gibson said with a sneer.

"Don't worry," Burton said as he sat down. "I finished your hopscotch squares first."

Before Gibson could think of a retort, Burton handed Haney a paper towel, then took it back when the man was done wiping his face and hands. He leaned back and put it in the garbage can, but not in the garbage bag. Instead, he placed it in an evidence bag he had taped to the inside of the rim before Haney had entered the room. He closed the evidence bag, then the garbage bag, and handed them to Gibson.

"Here, Frank. You always talk about how you want to clean up this town. Start with this room." Gibson looked as though he'd rather put the bag over Burton's head, but he snatched it away and slammed the door.

"Mr. Haney, you said that you and your wife spent the morning and early afternoon at the beach, then stopped on the way home to take some pictures from the lookout. Charlotte drove the entire time?"

"That's right," Haney said. His reddish face indicated to Burton that Haney wasn't too concerned about getting a sunburn. He recounted the entire story, obviously shaken by the event and needing to talk it through.

As he listened, Burton peered into his file at the accident

photographs, careful to keep them out of Haney's view. Charlotte's body, also tanned and sunburned, was damaged beyond recognition. However, with Ted at the scene as the accident occurred, no body identification was necessary. After fifteen minutes, Gibson returned and stood behind Haney. He had a printout in his hand, the results of the crime lab analysis of the paper towels. Gibson gave Burton a slight shake of his head. There was no zinc oxide or titanium dioxide on the paper towel Haney used.

Burton closed the file folder. "OK, Mr. Haney, I just have one more question. Where is Charlotte now, and why does she want us to think she's dead?"

How did Burton know?

Burton's File

The chemicals found on the steering wheel and driver's seat of Charlotte Haney's car, zinc oxide and titanium dioxide, are found in sunscreen. Whoever had been driving the car wore sunscreen. The paper towel Ted Haney used did not have any traces of those chemicals, which means that he did not apply the sunscreen to himself or another person. The body in the car was tanned and sunburned, too, signifying that no sunscreen had been applied recently enough to transfer onto the steering wheel and car seat. Charlotte Haney is alive and well somewhere, and she is wearing sunscreen.

With Deadliest Regards

"Well, this all looks very fancy and fun," Detective Gibson said as he entered the interview room. Burton was sitting across the table from Lionel Walker, an antiques dealer who happened to be wearing a nineteenth-century tuxedo and top hat.

"Yes," Burton said. "Mr. Walker is fancy, and I'm having fun, and now that you're here, we can add 'foolish' to the mix. Now I'm having even more fun. Are you having fun, Mr. Walker?"

"Most certainly not!" Walker sputtered. His white mustache bristled when he spoke, and Burton half expected an antique eyeglass to drop from his incredulous eye.

"You're not here to have fun," Gibson said, leaning onto the table. "You're here to confess to the murder of your sweetheart, Rebecca Shuman. So let's get it over with."

Walker refused to look at Gibson, and he spoke deliberately to Burton. "Good sir, would you be so kind as to remove this Neanderthal from my presence? He's making the very air unbreathable."

"Neanderthal?" Gibson said. "What's that, like a caveman? Listen here, frills, I wish we were in caveman times, because instead of a trial, you'd just get tossed off a cliff and forgotten. In fact, I think there's a cliff just down the road." Gibson took a step closer to Walker, who pulled his top hat off and held it in front of himself like a shield.

"Back, you cretin!" Walker shouted.

"All right, calm down," Burton said. "Mr. Walker, our forensic pathologist is examining the deceased Ms. Shuman right now. If there's anything you'd like to tell us before we find out for ourselves, it could help you out in court."

"The Lady Shuman and I do have a past," Walker said, keeping a wary eye on Gibson. "But we parted ways months ago and haven't spoken since then. I do pine for her, though, and send her antique faux flowers now and again. They were her favorite. I regret her passing as if it were my own."

Gibson rolled his eyes. "Where did you find this guy, Burton? The Melodrama Store?"

"Good one, Frank," Burton said. "You should write it down and use it again. You two play nice. I'm going to see how Dr. Crown is doing." As Burton left, he saw Gibson smile at Walker and thought he saw Walker begin to sweat.

Dr. Lauren Crown was the county's forensic pathologist, and that was just about all Burton knew about her. He had the feeling that if she could examine the bodies without leaving her garage, which she had converted into a home lab and library, she would. He entered the crime lab and found Mike Trellis assisting Dr. Crown in the examination of Rebecca Shuman.

"Hey, boss," Trellis said. "Check out her fingernails. Dr. Crown spotted it right away when she heard that Shuman had vomited several times before she died."

Burton looked at the corpse's fingernails and saw the white lines and horizontal ridges. "Arsenic poisoning?" he asked.

"Correct," Dr. Crown said without looking away from her microscope.

"Did hair analysis have traces of arsenic, too?"

"Yes," Crown said, and pointed to a printout on the table. Burton looked at the printout.

"Looks like she's been in contact with the poison for at least a few months, maybe longer," he said.

"Yes," Crown said, and picked up a bone saw.

Burton and Trellis waited for more comments from her, but she continued what she was doing without giving them a glance.

"Should we make small talk with her or just leave?" Trellis asked Burton quietly.

"I don't know," Burton answered. "Do you want to talk about advanced states of decomposition and what various forms of trauma can do to an eyeball?"

"No," Trellis said. "No, I don't. What about football?"

Burton considered it, then made a face. "Not likely," he said. "We'll probably have more luck talking with Gibson."

Burton and Trellis went back to the interview room, where Gibson was sitting on the table and Walker was sitting in the corner.

"Bad news, Mr. Walker," Trellis said. "You've been nailed."

What gave Walker away?

Burton's File

Walker mentioned that he had been sending artificial antique flowers to Rebecca Shuman since they broke up. As an antiques dealer, Walker would have known that many nineteenth-century items, including artificial flowers, playing cards, and hat liners, contained lethal amounts of arsenic. He sent the flowers to her knowing she would spread them around her apartment, surrounding herself with poison.

The Nose Knows

It was a chilly day, and Burton pulled his knit cap down over his ears as he approached the group of reporters. They were crowded around Carol Morrell, who was on the verge of tears. Her son, Brandon, stood next to her, trying to console his mother. Burton guessed his age to be thirteen.

"Please, if you know where my daughter is, call me, or the police, or anyone! She's only four years old! She —" Mrs. Morrell broke down then, the news cameras catching every second of her despair.

"All right, everyone," Burton said, "we're about to begin searching for Janie Morrell, so we need you to clear the area. Back to your vans and trucks, please."

Carol and Brandon stayed put, Carol wiping her eyes. "Please," she said. "Janie couldn't have gone too far, but Brandon and I can't find her. We stopped to pick up some fall leaves, and I took my eyes off her for a second, just a second. You don't think someone . . . took her, do you?" The tears welled back up, and she hid her face in her hands.

"We'll find her, Mrs. Morrell, don't worry," Burton said. "I'm Wes Burton, from the scene investigation department." He left out the word "crime," as he wasn't sure there was a crime yet, and the word sometimes upset people. "I'd like to establish a timeline before we get started. You left your home at 7:00 A.M. and stopped at this field to collect leaves around

8:00 A.M.; you noticed Janie was missing approximately ten minutes after that and called 911. Then at 8:23, the first officer arrived on scene. He asked you to stop talking to the reporters and make a statement, in case there was information that we could use to find Janie. It is now 8:37, so she's been missing for almost thirty minutes. Is that all correct?"

"I guess," Carol said. "I'm not sure about the times; things were crazy. I thought talking to the reporters would help, since more people would know she's missing and could look for her."

"Thank you, Mrs. Morrell," Burton said. "I'll go get my partner Ed, and we'll get to work finding your daughter." Burton made his way back to his truck, stopping on the way to check the Morrell minivan. The hood was cool to the touch, the driver's door open from when Carol made her 911 call. Burton found what he was looking for and headed for his partner.

"I checked your minivan and found a good scent article that will help us track Janie," Burton said when he returned.

"Your partner uses his nose to find people?" Brandon asked, temporarily distracted from his worry.

"Ed is a she, and she's a border collie," Burton explained. "Her name's short for Exhibit D. I adopted her after a trial a few years ago, and she does search-and-rescue with me. Here she comes. Would you like to meet her?"

Brandon nodded as Ed burst from the bushes, her coat tangled with burrs and her tongue flopping happily. Her orange search-and-rescue vest had bells sewn onto the back to help Burton follow her in the woods, and the chimes sang as she bounded toward the group.

"Come on, Ed!" Burton called. "Let's meet Brandon. We're going to find his sister Janie this morning!" Ed thought that was a great idea and let Brandon know by giving him a quick lick on the hand as he scratched her ears.

"Okay, Mrs. Morrell," Burton said. "You and Brandon can follow, but stay at least fifty yards behind me to keep the scent clean." With that, Burton turned his back and knelt next to Ed. He pulled a sealed plastic bag with something in it out of vest pocket 4, let Ed get a whiff, and off she went. Her nose worked furiously as she followed the scent that matched the item in the baggie.

"Here we go," Burton said. "Remember, stay behind me; I'll holler when Ed finds her."

Carol nodded, clearly anxious to see her daughter again. "Brandon, let's go get my mittens and your gloves. Mr. Burton should be far enough ahead by *then*." Her tone suggested that she resented being left out of the front lines, but Burton wasn't about to budge. He followed Ed, who was tracking the ground scent into the trees.

It only took twelve minutes for Ed to find Janie, who was sitting by the trunk of a tree waving a stick around. Burton arrived soon after and made sure the little girl was safe and warm. He radioed to the officers escorting the Morrells that Janie was safe and told them it was okay to come and get her.

"Oh, thank goodness!" Carol gasped as she lifted Janie off the ground and into a hug. The mother wore one red mitten on her right hand, which she took off to touch her daughter's face. "Thank you, Mr. Burton, and thank you, Ed. I don't know how long she would have been out here if you hadn't followed her scent!"

"You're welcome, Mrs. Morrell. But when your kids are safe, you'll have to come with us," Burton said as he pulled the baggie out of his pocket. In it was the other red mitten. "Ed didn't follow Janie's scent out here. She followed yours."

How did he know?

Burton's File

When the first officer arrived on scene, the reporters were already there, indicating that Carol Morrell had called them first, something a terrified mother would not do. If the van had been off for forty minutes, as Carol claimed, the hood would still be warm to the touch after driving for a full hour. That meant she had been stopped for a longer period of time. Long enough, in fact, for her to take Janie into the woods, tell her to stay there, and run back to her van and call the news channels and 911. Carol just wanted some attention — the judge will give her plenty.

The Scene's Abuzz

"Bug wants to talk to you," Detective Radley said to Burton.

"Do you have any idea why?" Burton responded as he packed away the last of his equipment. They had just finished processing a murder scene at the Rider's Lodge Motel, and Burton was hot and upset. The victim was unidentified, the room hadn't been rented to anyone during the time of the murder, and they hadn't been able to find much of anything in the way of evidence.

"Because you're the only one who can understand what he's talking about," she offered. Bug, or Burian U. Gorlach, was a recent immigrant to the United States from Russia. He owns Sensitive Cleaners, a company that specializes in the cleaning and decontamination of crime scenes when an investigation is complete. He was currently in room 41, where the murder took place.

"Good point," Burton said, and made his way to room 41.

"Ah, Wes Burtons, goods to see you!" Bug said, when Burton appeared in the doorway. He was standing near the middle of the room in a Tyvek suit, next to a large bloodstain in the carpet that looked like a rough sketch of Texas.

"Hello, Bug, good to see you, too. You must be hot in that suit. It's close to ninety-five degrees outside," Burton said.

"Yes, I am in fire," Bug said.

"What can I do for you?" Burton asked.

"I am thinking, I am good at cleaner of the stains of blood and filth, yes?" Bug said.

"One of the best I've ever seen," Burton said. And it was true; Bug was exceptionally thorough when it came to cleaning a messy crime scene.

"Da, da, but even I am not this good," Bug said, and pulled back the carpet. The underside of the carpet showed the back side of the bloodstain, indicating that the fluid had soaked through, but the concrete floor underneath was spotless.

"You didn't touch the concrete at all?" Burton asked, his interest immediately spiking.

"No, I just look at it, and it is already clean," Bug said. "I'm wishing my job is always this easy!"

Burton radioed to Detective Radley, and she arrived a few minutes later, along with the motel manager. "There's no blood on the concrete below the carpet stain," Burton explained. "I think the murder took place in another motel room, and the killer swapped out the carpet pieces. That's why there wasn't any evidence in this room. The way this place is laid out, every second room is identical." He stopped suddenly and looked at the manager. "How many rooms do you have?" he asked.

"Two hundred," the manager replied, wary of where the conversation was leading.

"So there are one hundred total rooms with the same floor plan as this one, leaving ninety-nine other possible murder scenes here," Burton said to Radley.

"Whoa, whoa, hold on there," the manager said. "I can't have you shutting me down while you peel up half of my carpets! Just removing the furniture will take all day!"

"That won't be necessary," Burton said. "Just open the other ninety-nine doors and wait about one hour."

Why didn't Burton need to pull up every carpet?

Burton's File

In the near 100-degree heat, the bloodstain on the concrete quickly attracted houseflies and blowflies. They are the first insects to arrive when a body starts to decay. Bug discovered the concrete was missing a bloodstain in room 41. Real bugs found the bloodstain for us in another room.

The Swirly Gig

"Sit down," Burton said for the second time. Across the interview table from him, twenty-one-year-old Ronnie Warren smirked and remained standing.

"You sit down," Ronnie said.

Burton frowned. "I am sitting down."

"Good for you."

"Do you consider this to be an actual conversation?" Burton asked.

"No, but you do."

"Sit down," said Burton.

"I don't have to sit down," Ronnie said. "I know my rights, and when my lawyer gets here, you'll be the one taking orders."

Detective Erin Radley moved around the table and stood next to Ronnie. She wore her favorite leather jacket, the dark, smooth leather a close match to her skin. Ronnie shifted slightly, apparently not very comfortable with a six-foot-one-inch woman looking down at him. She smiled, which made him more uncomfortable.

"Sit down, hon," she said. And he sat down.

"Wow," Burton said. "Are you going to put that in your book?"

Radley gave a modest shrug. "Why give away all my secrets?"

"What book?" Ronnie asked suspiciously.

"I'm compiling case studies on why criminals commit their crimes," Radley explained. "Perhaps you'd like to speculate on why you killed Tim Keenan?"

Ronnie paused, then a sly grin appeared. "Oh no, you're not going to trick me that easily!"

"Is that what you think we're trying to do?" Radley asked. "Trick you? Believe me, we don't want you to confess. We would rather see the long, drawn-out process of an indictment, a trial, appeals . . ."

"Don't forget the interrogations," Burton chimed in.

"Oh, yes, the interrogations," Radley said, and smiled at Ronnie again. The young man looked uncertain about the whole situation.

Before Radley and Burton could continue their conversation, Mike Trellis opened the door, followed by another man.

"This is Travis Beckman, the lawyer," Trellis said.

"That's how I'm introduced?" Beckman spat. "'The lawyer'? Like I'm some kind of professional wrestler?"

Trellis seemed to be distracted by this image, so Beckman turned his attention to Burton and Radley. "Whatever my client has said so far is inadmissible in court. He did not have proper representation at the time. And why is he wearing a jumpsuit? Has he been convicted already?"

"We confiscated everyone's clothes for examination," Burton said. "Mr. Warren is here regarding the death of Tim Keenan. They were teammates on a flag football team. They were playing a game at the park, when Ronnie and a few other players took a time-out to give Tim a swirly. He died."

"That's not true!" said Ronnie. "We were going to dunk him, and he just passed out —"

"Ronnie, hush," Beckman said, laying a hand on his client's arm.

Trellis held a folder in his hand and motioned for Burton to join him in the hall. Radley stayed in the room with the three men, still smiling, with her arms crossed.

"Crown just finished her exam," Trellis said. "Tim Keenan didn't drown; there was no water in his lungs. He died from postural asphyxia."

"His chest was compressed, making him unable to breathe?" Burton asked, scanning the notes in the folder.

"Righto," said Trellis. "She also found traces of a substance containing menthol. She took some photos—yeah, right there."

Burton pulled the images out of the folder. One showed Tim Keenan's back, with close-ups indicating the menthol substance around his kidneys. Another showed a pair of sweatpants, with the same substance on the back of the thighs.

"Are these Ronnie's pants?" Burton asked.

"Yessir," Trellis said.

"Well," said Burton. "We won't need a chair for this evidence; it'll stand up in court."

"Good deal," said Trellis. "So, did Ronnie flush his life down the toilet? Get it? Because they were giving the guy a swirly, and —"

"Yeah, I get it, Mike," Burton said, and left him in the hall.

"Am I going to miss the game this Friday? It's the league championship," Ronnie said to his lawyer.

"No, we'll be leaving right now, so this farce won't affect your playing time. Right?" Beckman directed this question at Burton, who shrugged.

"It shouldn't, as long as he can throw a football with handcuffs on."

How did Burton know?

Burton's File

Tim Keenan died from postural asphyxia, death by suffocation due to the position of the body or compression of the chest. Keenan also had menthol smeared on his lower back, a common ingredient in ointments for soothing muscle and joint pain, something a football player would have. The same substance was found on the back of Ronnie Warren's pants, indicating that he was sitting on Keenan's back while attempting to dunk his head in the toilet bowl. Keenan suffocated because his chest was pinned between Warren and the rim of the bowl.

Dirty Laundry

CSI technician Mike Trellis entered the interview room with a basket of clothes. His wire-frame glasses were crooked, and he set the basket down as soon as he could in order to straighten them. Trellis believed everything should be in its place all of the time. It was a philosophy that kept his laboratory neat, but it also made it easy for his peers to make him crazy. Peers like Wes Burton.

Burton dumped the clothes basket onto the interview table and scattered the laundry across the surface. Trellis clenched his jaw, his hand involuntarily twitching toward the clothes to put them back in the basket.

"Help me sort these, will you, Mike?" Burton asked, shoving the darks into one pile and the whites into another. Trellis began to fold one of the white T-shirts, and Burton snatched it from his hands and held it in front of Ben Reeves, the suspect in the interview chair.

"You say you were doing laundry when the robbery occurred," Burton said. "Did this shirt make it into the clean pile?"

"I already told you," Reeves sighed. "I washed everything. It's all clean. You took that shirt out of the dryer yourself, I saw you. Go ahead, smell it."

Burton put the shirt near his nose and sniffed. "Hmm. It is fresh like morning dew. What do you think, Mike?" Burton held the shirt for Trellis while the technician leaned closer.

"Smells like a meadow at dawn," Trellis said, his face unchanged.

"See?" Reeves exclaimed. "There's no way I could have robbed that greeting-card shop next door. I was too busy washing all my clothes."

"You could have left while they were in the dryer," Burton said. "Robbed the card shop, then returned to the Laundromat before we arrived."

"Yeah, you could have really taken that card shop to the cleaners," Trellis added. "Get it?"

"No, I don't get it," Reeves said. "I wouldn't have left my stuff there. Especially my soap; that stuff's expensive. People have snagged it before, and as you can see, it's not exactly a crime-free neighborhood."

Burton pulled a large orange container from the basket and set it in front of Reeves. The bottle read "Flow-Plus — Now with bleach alternative!"

"Is this your detergent? The detergent you used today?" Burton asked.

"Yeah, it's good stuff. You smelled it. It's good, right?" Reeves said.

"I'd use it," Trellis said as he turned off the overhead lights, leaving the room in darkness.

"That's a big compliment," Burton said in the blackness. "Mike is very picky about his soaps."

Reeves flinched as Trellis turned on his handheld UV light, casting a hazy purple glow throughout the room.

"This is ultraviolet light," Trellis said. "Sometimes

called UV for short, or black light. We use it to find traces of substances on fabrics and other surfaces. I'm just going to check your laundry and your hands real quick."

Trellis swept the light over the piles of laundry. The darks had a few pieces of lint that glowed dully, while the whites offered a flat grayish-white color.

"Nothing," the technician said, snapping the UV light off and the overheads back on.

"See?" Reeves said. "There's nothing. Can I go now?"

"Sure," Burton said. "You can go make your one phone call."

How did they know?

Burton's File

The detergent Reeves claimed to have used that day contained a "bleach alternative." When exposed to ultraviolet light, bleach, bleach alternatives, and white fabrics that have been washed in them, provide a bright glow. Reeves's whites were a dull gray, indicating that they had not been washed with that detergent in the recent past.

Reeves put his clothes in the dryer, went next door, and robbed the greeting-card shop. He was back with his laundry before the police arrived.

BADD: Burton Against Dead Drivers

"This is a tough tree," Trellis said, gazing up the four-foot-wide trunk to the top of the oak. It was at least fifty feet tall. The trunk was also stuck in the hood of a four-door sedan, the silver bumper bent around the tree like a piece of macaroni.

"It's probably seen worse than this during a windstorm," Burton said as he finished taking photos. "The driver, however, would disagree." The man slumped behind the steering wheel had been pronounced dead by the first emergency medical technicians on scene. Burton leaned into the front seat for a closer look.

"Broken nose, lacerations on the forehead, most likely from the impact with the windshield," he said. "No seat belt."

Trellis made a tsking sound, reprimanding the corpse for ignoring simple safety precautions. Burton panned his flashlight over the windshield. It was cracked in a spiderweb pattern, shatter lines spreading out from the center.

"Where's the blood?" he asked.

Trellis checked the same areas, then placed his beam on the driver's face. "A broken nose typically bleeds quite a bit," he said. "Could he have died instantly, stopping the heart and blood flow?"

"There would still be blood in the capillaries and

tissues," Burton said. "And if the impact with the windshield killed him, there would be blood on the glass for sure." He swept his flashlight down the body, stopping at the feet and the gas pedal.

"I've got some dust on and around the gas pedal," said Burton. He took some adhesive lifting tape out of vest pocket 7. He smoothed the lifting tape over the carpet below the pedal and sealed it away, then did the same on the pedal with another tape and sealed up that one. He held the two transparent sheets up for examination.

"Looks like bits of concrete," Trellis said.

"I agree, but we'll test it to make sure," said Burton. "Check the bottoms of his shoes for more." He handed Trellis two footprint-lifting tapes from pocket 21.

Trellis extended both of the driver's legs toward the pedals and shined his light onto the soles of his shoes. "I don't see any concrete, but it's hard to tell from this angle."

"Wait a minute," Burton said. "His feet don't reach the pedals."

Trellis looked at the man's feet, then the gas and brake pedals. "Huh," he said. "When it comes to driving this car, he comes up a little short. Get it?"

"Yeah, good one," Burton said. "Take some photos and a video of his feet and their distance from the pedals, then you can take the shoes off."

Trellis worked both cameras, then pulled the shoes off without untying them. He carefully pressed them onto the large lifting tapes. "I see some hair, what looks like possible dog poop, and various grit, but no concrete bits," he said.

"Call dispatch," Burton said. "Tell them this car accident just became the dump site of a murder victim."

"Are you sure?" Trellis said.

"Do you remember what I said about building a case with evidence?" Burton asked Trellis.

"Sure," Trellis answered. "It's like building a house, one piece of evidence at a time, using them like bricks until you have a solid foundation to base the case upon."

"Exactly," Burton said. "And right now, we need to find that first brick. And I mean an actual brick."

How did Burton know?

Burton's File

When a body dies, the blood begins to clot almost immediately. The lack of blood spatter on the windshield and the driver's body indicated that the wounds he suffered in the car accident were postmortem; he was already dead. When Trellis pulled the driver's feet toward the pedals to check for concrete bits, it was apparent that the driver could not have reached the pedals. That fact, combined with the traces of concrete found on the floor and the gas pedal, suggests that a brick was used to press the accelerator while the dead driver went along for the ride.

The Halloween Egg Scene

Burton sat on his front porch. Blood oozed from multiple gashes on his face and one eye dangled from its socket. A ninja, a hobo, and a princess walked up his steps, got one look at him, and stopped. For a moment, anyway — then the huge bowl of candy in his lap convinced them to approach.

"Trick or treat!" the hobo said, his worldly belongings stuffed into a handkerchief tied to a stick. The other two echoed him, and their father, who waited in the front yard, watched and smiled.

"I think I might have a treat or three for you," Burton said in a scratchy, sinister voice. "Chocolate or fruity?"

"Chocolate!" they all hollered. He gave them each a handful of assorted mini chocolate bars, then leaned in. They leaned back.

"Say, you kids haven't seen my pet alien around here, have you?" he asked.

"No," said the princess.

"Geez, I just saw him a minute ago," Burton said. "If he gets lost, I think my heart might break." Suddenly, a small, snarling creature burst out of Burton's chest, and he bellowed in agony. The three trick-or-treaters screamed and ran off the porch and into their father's arms, laughing hysterically. The father gave Burton a thumbs-up, which he returned as he reset the spring-loaded latex alien strapped to his chest. He helped himself to another chocolate bar, careful not to mess up his bloody face.

As soon as he heard Mrs. Wendell yelling four houses down the street, he was off the porch and on his way over to her house, with Ed right next to him on a leash. When he got to Mrs. Wendell's yard, he was careful to avoid the waist-high shrubs that ran along the street; her cats liked to use them as urinals. Ed hung back for a few sniffs but moved on after a light tug from Burton. Mrs. Wendell was standing in her front yard.

"What's wrong, Mrs. Wendell?" Burton said. "We heard you all the way from our place."

"Punks!" Mrs. Wendell said through gritted teeth. "They asked for candy, and when I gave them each one piece, they asked for more! I told them there were more kiddies on the way, so I had to make sure I had enough candy for them. And what do these kids do? They egg my house!" Burton could see the shattered shells and running yolks on her vinyl siding.

"Then they ran through my good bushes," Mrs. Wendell cried. She pointed to the shrubs along the road. "What I wouldn't give to have them come back for more candy! I'd give them garlic and liver wrapped in wax paper!"

"How about if I just get them to come back and clean up the mess they made?" Burton said.

"Oh, I'd make them do that, too," Mrs. Wendell said. "One of them left this plastic machete behind. Guess he couldn't hold it and pelt my house at the same time. Will it help you catch them?"

"What do you think, Ed?" Burton asked the perky-eared border collie. "Do you want to do some work?" Ed responded with furious tail wagging. Burton led her to the street side of the bushes. Burton held the plastic machete by the blade and offered her the handle, which she sniffed once. Then she was off.

Burton let her take her leash to its full length and trotted behind her. After a few lefts and rights, Burton spotted a group of teenagers at the end of the block. Ed led him right to them, then sat down and looked at Burton, which was her signal that she had found the source of the scent. He gave her a biscuit and scratched her ears.

"Excuse me," Burton said to the group and showed his badge. "I'm CSI Wes Burton. Can I ask you a few questions?"

"Um, I guess," said a werewolf.

"My neighbor's house just got vandalized by a group about your size," Burton said. "If it was you, and you come back and clean it up right now, we won't have to call the police."

"We didn't egg that lady's house!" protested a girl wearing a headset microphone and about seven pounds of makeup.

"What are you supposed to be?" Burton asked. "The person at the fast-food drive-through?"

"I'm a pop star!" she yelled.

"Oh, right," Burton said, and looked at Ed. She looked back at him and panted; she didn't see the resemblance either.

Burton pulled out a handheld black light, snapped it on, and stepped closer to the group. They stepped back in unison. "I'm just going to check for something," Burton said. "Hold still for three seconds." He swept the UV light across the group at their shins and saw greenish yellow streaks glowing on their pant legs.

"Cool! I'm radioactive!" said a zombie.

"Well, zombie," Burton said. "Call your undead, radioactive parents and have them pick you up at Mrs. Wendell's house in about an hour. It should take that long to clean up the mess you made."

How did Burton know it was them?

Burton's File

Ed tracking the scent to them was enough evidence to contact the police. However, it wouldn't convince the parents or get the kids to confess, so the situation required the use of an old detective's trick. At the mention that someone had vandalized a neighbor's house, one of the suspects responded with information she could only know if she had been there: Eggs were used, and it was a woman's house.

When the group fled the scene, they ran through Mrs. Wendell's "good" bushes, which contain a large amount of cat urine. Cat urine glows under black light, and the streaks on their pants showed they had run through the shrubbery. Case closed, eggs washed away, let's eat some candy.

Gamer Over

Burton and Detective Gibson stepped into The Gamer's Dungeon, and both immediately took off their sunglasses. "Won't be needing these in here," Burton said.

"Nah," said Tom "Nebular" Evans, the owner of the Internet café and multiplayer gaming center. "I keep it midnight dark in here around the clock. It cuts down on eye fatigue from monitor glare." He took a large gulp of some sort of coffee drink.

"What happens when people leave here after a few hours and hit the bright sunshine?" Detective Gibson asked.

"Oh, man, it's great," Evans said as he took them deeper into the Dungeon. "It's like watching vampires burn up from the sun. Except for the burning part. There's a lot of cringing and hollering. And you said 'a few hours.' Make it more like ten."

"Kids are in here for ten or more hours playing video games?" Burton asked, wishing he still had his sunglasses on so they could hide his surprise.

"Oh, yeah, and not just kids," Evans said with pride. "We have an over-thirty league that plays every Thursday, but they don't stay as late. Jobs." He said the word like it was his number-one competitor and gulped more coffee.

"Are these kids drinking caffeine the whole time they're here?" Burton asked.

"Some do, some don't," Evans said. "Some of them prefer energy drinks, which I also sell. Most like soda. I drink the hard stuff, double espressos. Make 'em myself." He tipped the mug to his mouth, emptying it.

"Let me guess," Gibson said, pointing into the far corner of the gaming room. "That's our dead guy." The people in the room had moved away from the figure slumped over his keyboard, but they hadn't stopped playing.

"Yeah, that's Trogdor139," Evans said. "No one knows for sure, but we think he's been like that for about an hour."

"Has anyone left this room since you discovered the body?" Burton asked.

"No," Evans said. "In fact, I think three more players have joined up since then." Gibson turned on his huge Maglite flashlight and lit up the immediate area while Burton took photos.

"Hey!" a voice shouted from close by.

"Shaddup!" Gibson offered as an apology.

Burton saw a black jacket hanging on the back of Trogdor139's chair and gently reached into the pockets, looking for identification. In the second pocket he found a prescription bottle.

"Lortox," Burton read. "This is medication for high blood pressure, or hypertension. The EMTs said they thought he died of a stroke, which would make sense if he had high blood pressure."

"So our guy had some stress from playing video games

all day," Gibson said. "Rough life. Looks like he wasn't too careful about it, though." Gibson indicated the six empty and one half-full espresso mugs next to Trogdor139.

"Yeah, he wasn't too mindful of his health," Evans said.

"Who was sitting closest to, uh, Trogdor?" Burton asked. "Before they found out he was dead."

"I think it was PixieDust56," Evans said. "She's over there. I'll go get her."

"Of course, PixieDustBall999 or whatever her name is," Gibson said to Burton. "Sounds like a robot. Can't wait to meet her."

Evans returned with a short, thin girl in a black T-shirt and maroon knit cap pulled down almost to her eyes. She wore headphones around her neck, and Burton could hear something loud and clanging coming from them.

"Hello, I'm Wes Burton, from the crime lab. Can I call you something besides PixieDust?"

"Laura," she said.

"OK, Laura, can you tell us anything about what Trogdor here was doing before he died?"

"Well," she said. "He's always a spaz, like pounding the mouse and keyboard, swearing and stuff. The newbies don't like to play when he's in the game. He's a camper and a TK'er."

"A what and a what now?" Gibson said.

Evans answered. "A camper is a player who finds a good hiding spot and sits there, not moving, killing players as they pass by. TK stands for Team Killer, someone who kills teammates on purpose. Trogdor139 was notorious for both, and I've had plenty of players leave because of him. He always taunted them because they couldn't kill him."

"Was he doing these things today?" Burton asked Laura.

"Oh, yeah, like big-time," she said. "And he was, like, shaking and acting all dizzy, like he kept wanting to tip over?"

"Is that a question or a statement?" Gibson asked.

"Um, a statement?" Laura said.

"Please continue, Laura," Burton said.

"Anyway," she said. "He was messing with his headphones for, like, a half hour. He said he couldn't understand what they were saying. Then he really started freaking out, like half of his body wouldn't work. Then he fell on his keyboard, and, like, died, I guess."

"Did you notice him getting worse as he drank these espressos?" Burton asked, pointing to the cups on the table.

"I guess, but he only drank decaf," Laura said. "He said caffeine was a crutch."

"Thank you for your time, Laura," Burton said. "You can go back to playing, but please don't leave just yet." When she left, Burton turned to Gibson. "I need to bag those coffee cups and the Lortox for testing."

To Evans, he said, "I think congratulations are in order. You finally killed Trogdor139."

How did Burton know?

Burton's File

Evans said that he made all of the coffee drinks himself, but when Gibson noticed the empty cups near Trogdor139, Evans did not mention that they were decaf, because they weren't. Trogdor139's behavior cost Evans customers and money. He switched the player to regular espresso in an attempt to disrupt his game. When the surge of caffeine increased Trogdor139's dangerously high blood pressure, he had a stroke and died.

Water You Trying to Prove

"Are you sure that's a person?" Trellis asked Dr. Crown.

"Female for certain, age is undetermined at this point," Crown answered. The body recovered from Two Mile Lake had been underwater for at least a few days, and the decomposition was advanced.

"I checked recent reports," Burton said. "There was a missing person report filed two days ago for Alyssa Taylor, who lives about a half mile from the lake."

"Do you have any DNA samples for comparison?" Crown asked.

"Her husband's on the way here with a hairbrush and her razor," Burton said. "It sounded like he'd rather keep hoping she's alive than get this kind of closure."

"Man, she's like a big sponge," Trellis said to no one in particular.

"Some people call it superhydration," Crown said. "Think about when you have your hands in water for an extended period of time. The thick skin on your palms and fingers swells up, but it's connected to a layer of skin beneath that doesn't swell, so the skin buckles, or prunes. Now imagine your whole body being submerged for days, and the different ways your tissues would react."

"Thanks, Dr. Crown," Trellis said. "Any more nightmares you'd like to plant in my head? How about telling me that the boogeyman is real?"

"The boogeyman isn't real," Crown said seriously, and picked up a cranium chisel.

"I appreciate that, Doctor," Trellis said, and looked back at the body. "Did she drown?" he asked, still unconvinced that the subject in front of him could have been a person.

"There was water in the air passages, lungs, and stomach," Crown said. "And hemorrhaging in the sinuses and lungs, indicating she was alive when she went into the water. I'm doing a complete toxicology exam on her just in case, including the water, to make sure she wasn't drugged."

"I think I hear the printer right now," Trellis said over his shoulder, practically sprinting away from the exam table. Burton was proud of the fact that Trellis hadn't vomited in the exam room yet, but today might be the day.

"Michael," Crown said. "Also check the lab to see if they've processed the water from her lungs."

"Here we go," Trellis said, walking back and concentrating intently on the printer paper. "The water has normal levels of calcium, magnesium, fluoride, and iron, with trace amounts of several other chemicals and elements. The lab also filtered the water from her lungs, and this was what they found." He held up a plastic bag with small particles in it, which Dr. Crown took as Trellis tried to focus on anything except the body.

After examining several samples under her comparison microscope, Crown looked at Burton with what he thought might be confusion, but since he'd never seen Dr. Crown confused before, he wasn't sure.

"These appear to be small segments of hair," she said. "All about an eighth of an inch long or less."

"Really?" Burton asked. "Her hair?"

"I don't think so," said Crown. "She's a natural brunette, and these are blond with a touch of red."

"Could they be —" Burton began but was interrupted by the exam room phone. He picked it up and said "Help! There are a bunch of dead people in here!" Crown shook her head.

"You know, I gave him that idea," Trellis said. "Do you get it? It's because —"

"Yes, I get it," Crown said. "It's because we're in a morgue. Morgues have dead people in them. It might have been humorous the first time, but it decreases in comedic value every time it is uttered."

"Oh," Trellis said. "I guess you do get it."

Burton made a hushing gesture so he could hear the desk sergeant at the other end of the line. "Go ahead, Sergeant," he said.

"Mr. Taylor is here with the hairbrush," the desk sergeant said from the lobby phone.

"Let me guess," Burton said. "He has strawberry blond hair, and he's clean-shaven."

"That's right, how did you know?" the desk sergeant asked.

"He fits the description of Alyssa's killer," Burton said. "Arrest him."

How did Burton know?

Burton's File

Alyssa Taylor was found in Two Mile Lake, but the water in her lungs contained fluoride, a chemical added to tap water. This meant that she was dumped in the lake after she was dead. The small hairs found in her lungs were her husband's shaving stubble, which had clung to the sides of the bathtub. When he drowned her in the tub, she inhaled the tap water and enough evidence to convict her killer.

Gesundheit Means "You're Guilty"

Dr. Crown leaned over the body of Gina Reardon on the examining table and spoke clearly for the boom microphone positioned above the work area.

"The marbled appearance of the skin indicates that the subject has been dead for at least four days; however, the presence of blowfly larvae suggests that the body has only been exposed to insects for sixteen to twenty-five hours."

"So Ms. Reardon was killed almost a week ago, but her body was kept indoors somewhere until a day ago?" Burton asked.

"That's correct," Crown said. "Insects don't lie." Burton noticed the whimsical way she said it, as if she admired their honesty. He appreciated their contribution to his investigations, but that was about as far as his feelings for insects went.

"Detective Radley was on scene where the body was found," Burton said. "I spoke to her on the phone, and she said there weren't any odd weather factors like extreme cold, so the insect timeline should be correct. The only reason I asked was because she was sneezing uncontrollably. I thought she might be in a freezer or something."

"I see." Crown said. "There is also a mold present on the body and clothing. Toxicology reports indicate that it is *Stachybotrysm,* a type of black mold that typically occurs on materials that contain fiber, such as cardboard, drywall, and wood, and are constantly wet."

Before she could continue, Mike Trellis poked his head into the examination room. "Hey, boss, they've rounded up the four jokers who were with Gina Reardon just before her disappearance. They all were at the same bar, one female and three males. All friends of hers. Well, except for one, I hope."

"Thanks, Mike," Burton said. "Can you ask Detective Radley to wait for me outside the interview rooms?"

"Sure thing. Do you want her to ask the questions while you give them the stink eye?"

"No, I want to ask them questions while Radley gives them the sniff test."

Why did Burton want Radley to sniff the suspects?

Burton's File

Detective Radley was sneezing over the phone while she was at the dump site of the body. Her sneezing was an allergic reaction to the black mold found on Reardon's body and clothes, which grew there while the body was being kept indoors. Whoever killed Reardon had a bad case of mold infestation at home, and when Radley sniffed the culprit, she started sneezing again. As Mike said after we arrested the killer, Radley was a "nose witness" to the crime.

Lying Without a Net

Burton approached the interview room and found Mike Trellis standing outside the door, nibbling on his pen. From the look of the plastic cap, Burton guessed it had been going on for quite a while.

"Are you going into the interview room?" Burton asked.

"Nope," Trellis answered.

"Is there a reason why?"

"Clown."

Burton paused. "Pardon me?"

Trellis finally took his eyes off the door and looked at Burton. "There's a clown in there."

"I know," Burton said. "He's Wammo the Clown. He's here for questioning about the death of Mad Kimo Kuhono, the Hawaiian tightrope walker who fell this afternoon. I just talked to the show promoter. He says he's ruined; Mad Kimo was the top attraction, and just about everyone in the stands leaves when his act is over. Now he claims they won't show up at all."

"Don't like clowns," Trellis said, going back to munching on the pen.

"Okay," Burton said. "Did you find out what that substance was on the top of Wammo's clown shoes?"

"Black sand," Trellis said, handing the printout to Burton. "It's unique to Wai'anapanapa State Park in Maui, Hawaii. That's the only place on earth you can find it."

"How did the black sand end up on the *tops* of Wammo's shoes instead of the soles?" Burton wondered aloud. "It must have fallen onto them."

"He's a clown," Trellis said, staring at the interview room door. "Laws of nature don't apply to him. Have you seen how many of them can fit into a car?"

Burton laughed, since Mike had finally made a good joke, but stopped when he realized that the technician wasn't kidding.

"Is the clown going to stay in there," Trellis asked, "or will he be wandering around scaring innocent technicians?"

"Go to lunch, Mike," Burton said, and entered the interview room. He heard Trellis's running footsteps as he closed the door.

"Hello, Wammo, I'm CSI Wes Burton."

"Hello," said Wammo, who sounded upset despite the huge grin painted on his face.

"Can you go over what happened again?" Burton said. "I just want to make sure I have the facts straight."

"I don't know why you're asking me," said Wammo. "I was in the food tent when Mad Kimo fell."

"I know, but it helps to get viewpoints from anyone in the area. Maybe you saw someone running out of the tent just before Mad Kimo fell?"

"Nope, nothing like that," Wammo said. "From what I heard, Mad Kimo stepped out onto the high wire, went a few steps and started to tip, then overcorrected with his balance pole and fell. They said a big black cloud puffed up when he hit the ground. I can't say for sure. I didn't go into the big top after he fell."

"Wait, back up. The balance pole," Burton said, flipping through his notes. "His partner Whooping Wendy said he made that pole when he was a child and never fell while he was using it. She called it his lucky pole."

"Not lucky enough, I guess," Wammo said, and honked his nose. "Sorry, habit."

"Yeah, I have habits, too." Burton said. "Like this one: You have the right to remain silent. . . ."

How did he know?

Burton's File

A tightrope walker's droopy pole is weighted at each end to lower the walker's center of gravity. The ends of Kimo's pole, which he built when he was a child in Hawaii, were filled with black sand found only in Maui, the same sand found on top of Wammo's shoes. If Wammo didn't go into the big top after the accident, the only way the sand could have gotten on his shoes is if he had let some of it out of the pole before Mad Kimo's act. Wammo was jealous of Mad Kimo's popularity, and he tampered with the balance pole, causing Mad Kimo to fall to his death.

There's No "Fun" in "Fungus"

"What's the story, Dr. Crown?" Burton said as he entered the autopsy room. He snapped on a vinyl glove.

"A story implies fiction. I deal in fact," she responded, without looking up from the body. Mike Trellis, who was assisting on the autopsy, snickered.

"Fair enough," Burton said. "What are the facts?"

"Brenda Thompson, age forty-three, diabetic. Her husband, Peter Thompson, brought her back from a camping trip after she began to exhibit symptoms of hypoglycemia. She was pronounced dead on arrival this morning at 9:36."

"Low blood sugar?" Burton asked. "Then why does she have signs of jaundice?" He had noticed the yellow shade of her skin as soon as he entered the room.

"That's why I authorized this autopsy," Crown said. "The husband didn't want to allow it, but I saw reasonable doubt about the cause of death."

"Wait a minute," Burton said. "Peter Thompson. The same Peter Thompson who runs that wilderness camp about fifty miles outside of town? Where the tourists can go and live off the land for a week, as long as they have five grand?"

"That's him," said Trellis. "He says they went on the camping trip to make up after a big argument. According to him, Brenda wanted to move back to the city so she could get back to her career. He's outside raising a fuss about how it's not natural to open a dead body. He said 'raccoons don't do autopsies!' How does he know?"

Burton and Crown looked at him, then at each other, and shrugged.

"The tissues in her esophagus and mouth are irritated," Crown continued, "indicating that she vomited recently. Quite violently, from the tissue damage. She's also severely dehydrated, which supports the vomiting, but has nothing to do with low blood sugar."

"Her skin does look pretty dry," Burton said.

"That's due in part to these," Crown said, holding up a box of alcohol wipes. "They used them to clean off; no showers in the wilderness. Good for cleanliness, but bad for moisturizing. Michael, is the blood analysis complete?"

Trellis walked over to the GC/MS equipment and checked the screen, then clicked PRINT. The results of Brenda Thompson's blood analysis purred out of the printer, and Trellis brought them over to Crown. She quickly found the culprits.

"Amanitin and phalloidin," she said.

"She was killed by aliens?" Trellis asked.

"Amanitin and phalloidin are poisons," Crown said. "Both are at highly toxic levels in the *Amanita phalloides* mushroom, better known as the 'death cap.'"

"They sound like real fungis," Trellis said, and looked around the room for applause. There wasn't any. "Get it? Fungis, fun guys?" Burton and Crown turned away from Trellis in an attempt to shut him out of the conversation.

"Did she eat some bad mushrooms by mistake?" Burton asked.

"There were no traces in her stomach or digestive tract," Crown said.

"Could she have barfed them all out?" Trellis asked, earning a stern look from Crown. "Sorry, vomited."

"There would still be traces in her intestines," Crown explained. "We only vomit what's in our stomachs, and amanitin usually takes six to fifteen hours before causing nausea. That's plenty of time for the contents of her stomach to be digested."

"There's a myth about poisonous mushrooms that says you can detoxify them by boiling them in water and vinegar," Burton said. "Any sign of vinegar at the campsite?"

"That myth is nonsense," Crown said. "The only way I've been able to extract the poison is with isopropyl alcohol, and no one would eat a mushroom after it's been soaking in that."

"Alcohol," Burton said. "Mike, tell the officers to arrest Peter Thompson for murder."

How did Burton know?

Burton's File

Peter Thompson was unhappy with his wife because she wanted to move back to the city, ending his business as a wilderness guide. He was familiar with the death cap mushroom and knew that one of its poisons causes hypoglycemia, a condition that can be fatal, especially to those with diabetes. He also knew that the poisons can be extracted using alcohol and that absorbing the tainted mixture through the skin can be as toxic as eating the fungus. He thought the poisoned alcohol wipes he made would allow him to kill his wife and get away clean, but they ended up proving him dirty.

The Tanning (Death) Bed

The room was small, and Burton imagined the home owner had a hard time getting the large tanning bed through the door. The bed was now turned off, with the body of Clive Lentil in it. Lentil wore shorts and a set of tanning goggles, which looked like small plastic spectacles. Every inch of exposed skin was bright red.

"Man, I've heard these things are bad for you, but this is out of control," Trellis said, tripping on Burton's foot.

"Hey, watch it," Burton said. "It's like having a meeting in a phone booth in here. What did this room used to be, a closet?"

"Looks like it," Trellis said. "I don't see any heat registers or vents, so no one was worried about keeping the room warm or cool."

"That's why Lentil used that kerosene heater in the corner," Radley said as she entered. "Mrs. Lentil says he kept it running so the bed wouldn't be cold when he got in it. Guess he couldn't wait for the bulbs to warm it up. Ow, that's my elbow."

"Your elbow? What about my ribs?" Trellis said. He would have rubbed the sore spot but didn't have enough room. "So this guy died because he wanted to be tan? Cause of death: vanity."

"That may not be the case," Burton said. "There is a condition called seasonal affective disorder; the most common type is also called winter depression. Doctors aren't certain, but it's probably caused by the body's reaction to a lack of sunlight. Some people use tanning beds during the winter months to get a dose of fake sunlight, but it's not a recommended treatment; the UV rays are too strong."

"Great, so now we add clinical depression to the mix," Trellis said. "What's behind door number three, massive gambling debts?"

"You're on my foot again, Mike," Burton sighed.

"Who had garlic for lunch?" Radley asked.

"Sorry," Trellis said.

"Okay," Burton said, "Mike, if you're done taking photos and video, step outside for a bit. Detective Radley, please see if Mrs. Lentil still has the instructions for the tanning bed. I want to see if her husband put in the wrong type of bulbs."

"Got it, boss," Mike said.

"I'll be in the kitchen," said Radley.

Alone, Burton still thought the room was too small to work in, but he'd been in tighter spaces before. He knelt next to the tanning bed and, with a gloved hand, pulled the tanning goggles off of Lentil's face. The eyelids beneath were the same bright red as the rest of Lentil's skin. Burton put the goggles in an evidence bag from vest pocket 9 and sealed it. He took a close-up photo of the eyelids.

"We might have a problem," Radley said from the doorway.

"No instructions for the tanning bed?"

"Worse. Mrs. Lentil's already on the phone with her

lawyer, talking about suing the manufacturer for killing her husband."

Burton shook his head. "Tell her to drop that case and start one against the kerosene heater, whoever built this room, and Mr. Lentil's red blood cells."

How did Lentil die?

Burton's File

While the bright red color of Mr. Lentil's skin originally indicated that he'd been overexposed to the tanning bed's heat, the fact that his eyelids were also red suggested another cause of death. They would not have been burned with the tanning goggles on. When too much carbon monoxide is inhaled, the body suffocates and bleeding occurs under the skin, resulting in a flushed appearance that is quite similar to a sunburn. In the small, unventilated tanning room, the carbon monoxide created by the kerosene heater would have quickly rendered Mr. Lentil unconscious, and he suffocated soon after that.

The Sale of a Lifetime

The yellow CRIME SCENE — DO NOT CROSS tape was already up when Burton arrived. He reluctantly put his custom-made tape back in vest pocket 2. It sometimes lightened the mood of witnesses and helped them talk about what they had seen. He crossed the parking lot to a blue four-door sedan with a dead man in the driver's seat.

"Greetings, Detective Radley," he said. She was peering into the driver's window, pointing out areas that she wanted CSI technician Mike Trellis to photograph and video.

"Hello, Burton," she said. "We have one victim, cause of death a gunshot wound to the head." If Radley found the scene disturbing or gross in any way, her voice did not suggest it.

"Do we have the shooter?" Burton asked.

"No, but we do have an eyewitness. The driver was a soap salesman, and his passenger was a salesman-in-training." Radley pointed toward a man sitting about twenty yards away on the bumper of a police car. His suit coat was off and his tie undone. He had blood smeared across his face and clothes and looked as though standing up would be bad for him.

"The trainee, Daniel Hawes, went to get some take-out from the deli around the corner while our victim, William Torwell, stayed in the car to fill out some paperwork," Radley said. "Hawes says he was followed from the deli by a man,

63

and when Hawes got back in the passenger seat, the man approached the driver's window and told Torwell to give him the keys. Torwell refused, so the man shot him and ran away."

"Any good material for your book on why criminals do what they do?" Burton asked her.

"I don't think so," Radley said. "Pretty typical shoot-and-run, if it ends up being like Hawes claims."

"Did Hawes get a good look at the shooter?" Burton asked as he looked into the car.

Radley shook her head. "He said he didn't want to make eye contact with him, so he didn't look at his face."

"Smart, I guess," Burton said. "Some animals, including humans, consider eye contact to be a challenge sometimes." The interior of the car was a mess, with blood spattered onto nearly every surface. The passenger seat and window were covered. The shot had come from the driver's window and the bullet had exited through the back of Torwell's head.

"Where did the bullet end up?" Burton asked. Torwell was slumped over the steering wheel, but Burton pictured him sitting up when he was shot. "Mike, are you done taking pictures? I'd like to correct Mr. Torwell's posture."

"All set," Trellis said. "I need to take some photos of the paperwork Torwell was filling out anyway, and it's in his lap."

The two of them eased Torwell's body into an upright position, as he would have been at the time of the shooting. Burton found the entrance wound, just above the left ear, and inserted a trajectory dowel. The long rod followed the path of the bullet as it entered the skull, indicating the location of the gun barrel. He did the same for the exit wound, the rod extending out and tracing the path of the bullet once it left Torwell's head.

"The bullet was fired from slightly above and in front of Torwell," Burton said. "It exited near the bottom of his skull and went into the backseat. Mike, let's try to recover the slug."

"I'm on it," Trellis said as he put on an extra pair of gloves. "The paperwork is a trainee evaluation form for Hawes. Looks like he wasn't doing very well; Torwell recommended him for warehouse duty."

"There is stippling around the entrance wound, so the gun was within two feet of Torwell's head when it was fired." Burton indicated the small abrasions on Torwell's face and neck. The abrasions were caused by unburned gunpowder and small pieces of metal that exited the gun along with the bullet.

"Must have been loud in the car," Trellis remarked, while he searched the backseat for a bullet hole.

"I agree," Burton said, and turned toward Daniel Hawes. He was still sitting on the car bumper and looking at the ground.

"Mr. Hawes?" Burton said at normal conversation volume.

Hawes looked up immediately, still in shock but eager to help out. "Y-yes?"

Burton walked over to the salesman-in-training. The

smeared blood on the man's face and clothes made him look even more traumatized. "I'm Wes Burton, CSI. I hope you sell soap better than your story, because I'm not buying it."

How did he know?

Burton's File

Daniel Hawes claimed that he was in the passenger seat when Torwell was shot. If that were true, the passenger seat and window would have been mostly clean rather than completely spattered with Torwell's blood. Hawes did have blood smeared on his face and clothes, but there was no spatter on him, indicating that he was not in the passenger seat when Torwell was shot.

A gunshot is loud, typically around 140 decibels (normal conversation is about 60). A gunshot inside a car is deafening. If Hawes had been in the car when Torwell was shot from less than two feet away, he would not have heard his name from twenty yards away.

Hawes knew that Torwell was giving him a bad review and shot him for it. He dumped the pistol, got into the passenger seat, and smeared some blood on himself, then called the police. At least prison doesn't have warehouse duty.

The Death of the Potty

"This is either the cruelest murder," Burton said, "or the dumbest case of accidental death I've ever seen." Burton, Trellis, and Detective Gibson were looking into the hunting cabin's outhouse, where the jeans-covered legs of Randy Banks were sticking up out of the toilet. His hunting boots were on his feet, and Burton could clearly read the Lumberland brand name on the soles.

"Either way, something about this case stinks," Trellis said. "Get it? Because of the poop."

"You're fired," Gibson said.

"Don't fire him yet, Frank," said Burton. "We might need someone to go into the outhouse to look for evidence."

"I hope you have a wet suit," Gibson told Trellis, who wasn't laughing anymore. Gibson turned to Burton. "So this guy drops something into the john, goes in after it, gets stuck, and dies?"

"Pretty much, if that's what happened," Burton said. "Sewer gas is made up of hydrogen sulfide, carbon monoxide, and methane. When you inhale it, it takes the place of the oxygen in your blood, and your cells don't get any oxygen. It's a very smelly way to suffocate. We can get a blood sample at the lab. If he has high levels of sulfide, we can conclude he died that way."

"Who found him like this?" Trellis asked.

"One of the other hunters," Gibson said. "There are three more of them in the cabin right now. They said they all had a few beers, went to bed, and woke up this morning with no sign of Banks. One of the guys heads for the bathroom and finds him like this. Not really the way you want to be remembered."

"What do you think he dropped down there that was so important?" said Trellis.

"Only one way to find out," Burton said. He pulled a filtered mask out of vest pocket 15 and snapped it over his nose and mouth. "Mike, you take the left side, I'll take the right. We need to pull the body up as far as we can, then out." Burton was careful not to slip on the muddy ground outside the outhouse. He was going to get dirty at this scene, but the longer he could put it off, the better.

"Oh, man," Trellis said, also trying not to slip as he entered the outhouse. "If I pass out, you guys have to promise not to take pictures of me."

"I promise," Burton said. Trellis looked at Gibson, who looked back and said nothing.

"OK, on three," said Burton, as he gripped Banks's belt with his right hand and wrapped his left arm around the body's right leg. "One, two, hold it!"

Trellis almost pulled up on the body, let go just in time, and stumbled out of the small outhouse into Gibson's arms. Gibson tossed him aside and looked at Burton.

"What is it?" he said.

Burton pointed to the small of Banks's back, where his

shirt had been hiked up when Burton grabbed his belt. The skin was a dark purple.

"Hold those three hunters for questioning, and seal off the cabin. This man didn't die in the outhouse."

How did Burton know?

Burton's File

The dark purple color of Banks's back is called lividity, which is caused by gravity pulling blood to the lowest areas of the body after the heart stops. In Randy Banks's case, he was lying on his back when he died, and stayed that way for at least six hours. (If Banks had been rolled onto his left side within those six hours, the blood would have settled there.)

If the other hunters were telling the truth, the lividity in Banks's body would have been in his head, arms, and shoulders, as those were the lowest parts of his body. In addition, the soles of his hunting boots were clean, even though the ground outside the outhouse was extremely muddy. Banks didn't walk into the outhouse, he was carried. Trellis is right; something does stink about this case.

The Bitter Taste of Guilt

Burton walked into the bar and immediately spotted Detective Radley and Mike Trellis near the group of people being held for questioning. He approached the two of them and asked the bartender for a cup of coffee.

"A man walks into a bar," Trellis said. "He orders a cup of coffee, because it's two in the morning, and then . . ." he looked at Burton expectantly, waiting for him to finish the joke. Burton did.

"He asks the two people who are already there why he had to get out of bed at 2:00 A.M. for some lady who had her purse stolen in a bar," he said.

"Ha! I love that one!" said Trellis.

"You're here because of what was in the purse," Radley said. "This is Julie Lanier, the owner of the purse." She gestured toward a woman nearby, who stepped into the group.

"Did you find my purse yet?" she asked Burton. The smell of alcohol on her breath was overwhelming.

"It's two in the morning," Burton said. "I haven't even found my face yet. But I did find some breath mints." He took a tin out of vest pocket 11 and offered her one. She took three and managed to get two in her mouth.

"What was in your purse, Miss Lanier, that is causing so much trouble?" Burton asked.

"A great big gun," she said, and pointed her finger at him with her thumb up. "Bang bang!"

"I see," Burton said. "Can you tell me what happened?"

"I can fill you in," Radley said, making Burton very happy. "Miss Lanier was talking with a man in a dark area of the bar. Because of the lighting and her intoxication, she doesn't remember what he looked like and can't pick him out of the group we have over there." Radley pointed to the dozen men standing around the other end of the bar, being watched by two uniformed officers.

"Those guys all look completely different," Burton said. "How can she not pick him out?"

"It was dark, people have to lean way in next to your ear to talk because of the loud music," Trellis said. "You know how it is."

"No, I don't," said Burton. He looked at Radley. "What happened next?"

"The guy she was talking to said something rude, so she threw her drink in his face," Radley said.

"Yeah, I doused him good!" Lanier said. "All over his shirt and everything!"

Radley waited to see if the commentary was done, then continued. "He shoved her back, grabbed her purse off the bar, and took off. The doorman said no one has left the place through the front, and all the other exits are alarmed. So the thief stashed the purse somewhere inside, and he might have the gun on him right now. Problem is, we don't have enough probable cause to search all of them. We need to narrow down the suspect list before we can search anyone."

"Can you smell them?" Burton asked. "Find out which one smells like he had a drink thrown in his face?"

"They all smell that way," Trellis said. "And a few of them smell like they had some wet garbage thrown in their hair." He looked at the group of men. "It's called a shower, guys!" They smiled and nodded back, having no idea what he said. One of them waved.

"What drink did you throw in his face?" Burton asked Lanier.

"Huh?" she said and wobbled. "Who threw a drink in my face?"

Burton frowned.

"I can answer that," the bartender said as she set Burton's coffee down. "Miss Lanier was drinking gin and tonics all night."

"You're absolutely certain of that?" Burton asked.

"Absolutely," the bartender said. "I can print her tab right now."

"Do it," Burton said, and took a small black light out of vest pocket 25. "As for our suspects, line them up. I'll let you know who to question in less than a minute."

How is Burton going to identify the thief?

Burton's File

Miss Lanier threw a gin and tonic on the thief's face and shirt. The bitter taste in tonic water is caused by quinine, a natural product found in the bark of the cinchona tree. Quinine also glows brightly under ultraviolet light, or black light. By scanning the group of men with the UV light, it was easy to find the perpetrator.

The Bathroom Brawl

"I already told you, it was self-defense," Al Williams said, and he was right. He had already told them: four times at the scene, twice in the car, and three times since he'd sat down in the interview room. Burton was beginning to wonder if Williams was trying to convince them or himself.

"Definitions of self-defense can vary," Detective Gibson said, pacing behind the seated Williams. "Maybe you thought he was going to pop you in the face, so you hit him first. Or maybe he said he was going to give you a whuppin', so you got scared and threw the first punch."

"No, no," Williams said, shaking his head. "We were in the bathroom arguing over this girl Stacy, and Trevor started to push me, then he hit me in the eye." Williams indicated the swelling there as evidence. "So I blocked the next few strikes — I've had some martial arts training — and punched him in the stomach. That slowed him down, but he was still coming after me, so I kicked him in the head."

"And killed him," Burton added.

"In self-defense," Williams added to that.

"I've never kicked anyone in the head," Gibson said, seeming a bit sad about it. "How do you get your leg that high?"

"Training, like I said." Williams shrugged.

Burton tuned out the circus for a moment and studied the crime scene photographs. One shot taken from the doorway interested him. The deceased Trevor was on the floor of the bathroom. The room measured five feet wide by eight feet long. It was a small room, with the urinal and toilet on the right wall and the sink and paper towel dispenser on the left.

Another image, a close-up of Trevor's head, showed blood spatter on the floor. The drops of blood made dotted "i" shapes pointing away from his head. Burton looked up from the photos to see Gibson taking off Williams's handcuffs.

"Show me how you kicked him," Gibson said, stepping away from the table. Williams stood up and measured the distance between him and Gibson, then made sure he had enough room on the sides. Then his right leg swung from his side in a long arc over the table, and passed about six inches in front of Gibson's face.

"Man, oh, man, that would hurt!" Gibson said, smiling. "So that's the same kind of kick you used on Trevor, with your leg coming around the side like that? What's that called?"

"It's a round kick, or a roundhouse kick, depending on the training," Williams said.

"I hate to interrupt the lesson," Burton said, "but is there a name for kicking someone in the head when they're already on the ground?"

How did Burton know?

Burton's File

The size of the room was the first tip, especially after Williams demonstrated the kick he claimed to have used. The small bathroom would not have allowed him to get his leg fully extended at his side. His foot would have hit the wall or toilet before he hit Trevor.

The bloodstain pattern, a series of dotted "i" shapes, indicated that the blood hit the floor at a small angle, close to 10 degrees. This puts Trevor's head at or near the floor when it was struck. If Trevor had been standing, as Williams claimed, the blood from his wound would have hit the floor at 90 degrees as it dropped, leaving round spatters. Williams knocked Trevor to the floor and then kicked him, a clear case of homicide.

You Have the Write to Remain Silent

Burton and Trellis arrived at the bank just before the press did, which made Burton happy. He didn't appreciate having to answer questions when he still had so many himself. Trellis liked being on the news. He claimed his appearances "let the ladies know I'm around."

"Hey, they're giving out free toasters when you open a savings account," Detective Radley said when she spotted them.

"I don't know how to make toast," Burton replied. "What do they give you when you rob the place?"

"A minimum of five years in prison," Radley said. "We have a suspect inside, but he says it wasn't him. Imagine that."

"Hey, Burton, I think I have an artist's sketch of the robber," Trellis said, holding up a fast-food napkin he'd grabbed in the truck. Burton looked at it. It was a crude drawing of a man in a ski mask, his eyes crossed and a speech bubble off to the side that read *Stick 'em up!*

"Get it? Because that's how he looked when he robbed the place," Trellis said.

"Hey, someone wants you over there," Burton said, pointing to the other side of the bank lobby.

"Who?"

"Everyone over here," Burton answered and turned to Radley. "Where did they find the suspect?"

"He was out of breath, sitting in a booth at a diner three blocks away," Radley said. "The cook called 911 when he heard that the bank had been robbed. He noticed that our suspect was wearing long sleeves, long pants, and had a knit cap sticking out of his pocket in the middle of July."

"He ran from the bank robbery? Guess he didn't buy the right getaway shoes," Trellis said.

"Regardless," said Radley. "He's sticking to his story that it wasn't him. Here's the note the robber used." She handed Burton a plastic bag with a white piece of paper in it. The writing on it was printed by hand.

He read aloud: " 'GIVE ME ALL THE MONEY AND NO ONE GETS HURT.' Quick and to the point, I guess," he said. The letters were written in ink. The lines were smeared, but they could still be read. "Let's go talk to our runner."

The suspect, Shawn Davis, was sitting at the bank manager's desk, surrounded by police officers. Burton sat across from him and introduced himself and Trellis.

"Now, we're going to do a writing exercise," Burton said, pulling a pen out of vest pocket 6 and a pad out of pocket 3. "I'd like you to write the following: 'Give me all the money and no one gets hurt.' "

Davis took the pen in his right hand and spun the paper so that the lower left corner was pointing toward him. He wrote the phrase in cursive, hooking his wrist and sliding the

78

paper from right to left as he went. When he finished, he pushed the sheet back to Burton, a small smile on his lips.

"I'm telling you, you got the wrong guy," he said. Burton looked at the writing. It was a barely legible mush. The letters slanted backward, as though they were being pulled at the bottom.

"This looks like 'Big me att the monkey and no one gels kurl,'" he said, offering it to Trellis, who shook his head.

"It looks like he wrote it with his foot," he said.

"Is sloppy handwriting a crime?" Davis asked.

"No, but obstructing a criminal investigation is," Burton answered and slid the pad back to Davis.

"Now write it with your left hand, the one you usually use, and tell me where you stashed the money."

How did Burton know Davis was left-handed?

Burton's File

At an early age, most left-handers are taught to spin the writing paper slightly counterclockwise so the lower left corner is to the right of their midsection and to slide the paper from right to left as they go, to prevent their left hand from smearing the letters (as in the robbery note). Though this is intended to keep the writer from hooking his or her wrist, if they aren't corrected, many writers will still hook in order to see what they are writing. Also, when a left-handed writer attempts to write like a right-hander, it can result in "backhand"

79

script, where the letters slant backward and become nearly illegible.

Davis showed all of these tendencies when he wrote the note with his right hand, his habits proving he was left-handed, since right-handed writers do not need to make any of those adjustments.

The Cracked Safe Cracks the Case

"Wow, this guy is good. No explosives or torches, and he didn't have to peel the sides off to get in," Burton said. He was examining an open safe in the crime lab, brought in by Trellis and three other helpers.

"What did the owner of the jewelry store say?" Burton asked Detective Radley.

"It was fine when he left work last night, and this is how he found it this morning. His inventory shows that there was close to five hundred thousand dollars' worth of diamonds and other stones in there." Radley, who didn't wear jewelry, sounded insulted that something so small could cost so much.

"So this case won't be making an appearance in your book?" Burton asked.

"I already know the *why* of this one," Radley muttered. "Greed. We don't need any more insight into why people steal. It's because they're lazy, desperate, cruel, and/or have a disorder. Believe it or not, I'm actually more interested in the *how* for this case."

Burton nodded approvingly, then took a brush out of vest pocket 16 and silver latent print powder out of pocket 22 and began dusting the door of the safe for fingerprints, knowing that there wouldn't be any. A safecracker this good would definitely wear gloves, probably two pairs. A series of whorls did appear near the dial, but it was too big to be a fingerprint.

"We do have a Mr. Horace Dubois in custody," Radley said. "An eyewitness saw him leaving the building around three this morning."

"What kind of eyewitness is out and about at that time of night?" Burton asked. "A vampire?"

"No, she's an early shift waitress at a diner across the street from the jeweler's," Radley said. "She said the guy had been spending time in the restaurant, drinking coffee and writing in a notebook. She thought he was some kind of author, then she sees him leaving the jeweler's at three in the morning. When she saw the black-and-whites there around six, she flagged one of the officers down and told him what she saw. I showed her some photos of known safecrackers, and she picked out Horace right away."

"Sounds pretty good," Burton said.

"Yeah, except she won't testify," Radley said, not bothering to hide her disgust.

"Don't tell me," Burton said, still looking at the safe. "She doesn't want the Mafia to come after her."

"Too many movies, too much TV," said Radley. "She thinks she's going to need witness protection, relocation, plastic surgery, new shoes . . . I told her that Horace was working alone, otherwise he wouldn't have been walking away from the jeweler's."

"And she still won't testify?" Burton asked.

"Not a chance. We were lucky to get her to come down and look at the photos. I had to let her wear my coat and motorcycle helmet as a disguise."

"Maybe we don't need her," Burton said. "I'm going to fume this safe with cyanoacrylate. Can you give me a hand rolling it into the booth?"

He and Radley rolled the cart and safe into the Plexiglas tank. Burton placed a few drops of superglue into the tiny dish on top of the tank's heater. He closed the airtight door and turned on the heater and small fans inside the tank. Once the glue reached the boiling point, its fumes circulated throughout the tank and stuck to any trace of amino acids, fatty acids, sweat, or other substances left behind by human touch.

"There we go," Burton said, pointing to the whorls he'd spotted earlier. The glue's fumes had found them as well, creating a sticky white material along the ridges of the seashell-shaped print. "Don't save a seat for this evidence; it'll be standing up in court."

"That looks a little big for a fingerprint," Radley said.

"Who said anything about a finger?" Burton replied, and headed for the interview room, his digital camera in hand.

"Hello, Horace," he said. "I'm here to take your picture for the mug shot yearbook." He walked around the table to Horace's left side. "Face front please," he said. When Horace did, Burton took a close-up of his left profile and headed for the door.

"Don't you want a shot of my pretty face, too, before I ditch this place?" Horace asked.

"I'll see enough of that in court," Burton said, and closed the door.

Why did he want a shot of Horace's profile?

Burton's File

Horace Dubois was very careful to avoid leaving fingerprints behind, but he didn't think about another unique body part that could identify him: his ear. When he pressed against the safe's door to hear the lock tumblers, he left a perfect print of his left ear, a body feature that scientists have shown is never duplicated.

The Rules of Drool

"Your dog ate my cake," Scott said.

"Yeah, she's in trouble," Danny added. Burton's nephews were out of breath from running over to give him this news. The family reunion had been pretty uneventful until now. Burton considered Uncle Stan's belch at the dinner table the highlight.

"Are you sure?" he asked the boys.

"Yup," said Danny, the younger of the two. Both of the boys were dirty from playing, but the dirt on Danny's good pants was serious enough to cause problems when his mom saw it. "We were playing catch, and I threw the ball over the fence. Scott went to get it, and when he got back the cake was gone."

"What kind of cake was it?" Burton asked.

"Chocolate with chocolate frosting," Scott said. He sounded like he'd lost a close friend.

"If she did eat it, we need to get it out of her stomach," Burton said, already moving. "Chocolate is very bad for dogs. She could die from eating it."

"Really?" Danny asked, jogging to keep up. "What does she have for dessert?"

"Oh, green beans, pumpkin, sometimes a beef tendon. It depends," Burton said.

"Gross," said Danny and Scott.

In the backyard, Burton found Ed lying under the picnic

table. There was a white paper plate faceup on the ground, but she seemed more interested in a bee that was buzzing around her tail.

"Come here, Ed," Burton said. She trotted over to him, tail swishing, and sat at his feet as he knelt down. He checked her teeth and gums for traces of chocolate.

"I don't see anything," he said to the boys. "No grass either. Some dogs will eat grass to make themselves vomit."

"Gross," said Scott again.

"How come cows don't throw up when they eat grass?" Danny asked.

"Where do you think milk comes from?" Burton said.

"Ohhh! Nasty!" The boys almost fell on the ground giggling.

"I'll be right back. Ed, you stay," Burton said. He returned from his truck with a bottle of hydrogen peroxide and a miniature ultraviolet light. The boys were pretending to eat grass, throw up, then drink it. Ed was blinking and enjoying the warm sun on her back, sticking out her pink tongue.

Burton went to the paper plate and knelt. There were a few cake crumbs still attached and a streak of frosting near the edge. He switched on the UV light and ran it over the plate, the fluorescent bulb about an inch above the surface.

"What are you doing?" Scott asked, forgetting about his cow imitation.

"Dried body fluids will light up when illuminated with

UV light, except blood, which looks black," Burton said. "If there is any saliva on this plate, it will glow when I run this light over it."

"I see some right there!" Danny said, pointing toward the plate.

"That's frosting," Burton said.

"What about that?" Danny asked, his finger moving across the plate.

"That's a piece of leaf," answered Burton.

"Hey! Get away!" Danny burst out, jumping back from the plate. Ed's friend the bee was buzzing next to Danny's pant leg, trying to land on his dirt stain. Scott ran to the other side of the picnic table.

"Get away, bee!" Danny yelled, swiping at the insect.

"Don't swat at it," Burton said softly. "You'll only scare him." He brought the UV light over to the bee, which drifted away from Danny and toward the light.

"Bees are attracted to ultraviolet light," Burton said. "Some flowers have patterns that are only visible under UV light. The patterns help the bees find the center of the flower, where the pollen and nectar are." He slowly took the light over to a flower bed, where the bee landed on a sunflower and got to work.

"So," he said, switching off the light. "Danny, I think you owe Ed an apology, and your brother a piece of chocolate cake."

How did Burton know Danny ate the cake?

Burton's File

The crumbs and frosting on the plate were the first indicators that Ed did not eat the cake. A dog would have licked the plate clean, leaving no crumbs and plenty of saliva behind. The UV test showed no saliva on the plate.

The stain on Danny's pants, originally thought to be dirt, was chocolate. Danny wiped his hands after he ate the cake. The bee detected the sugar and buzzed in for a closer look. Danny waited until Scott left to retrieve the ball that went over the fence, then ate his piece of cake.

The Shocking Truth

When Burton arrived at the construction site, Detective Radley already had the electricians sitting in the break area. Don Evans, master electrician, lay two stories up from where they sat. He had stepped off a two-man lift and fallen sixty-seven feet, dying upon impact. Radley met Burton before he reached the group of men.

"They're all pretty upset," she said. "It's dangerous work, and something like this doesn't make it any easier. Especially when it happens to someone like Evans, who's been doing it for twenty years."

"So he just jumped?" Burton asked.

Radley flipped her notebook open. "Witnesses say at around 8:45 A.M. — they know the time because that's fifteen minutes before break — Evans was in the two-man lift with Kevin Randolph. They were working on a one-hundred-amp electrical panel. Randolph said that Evans jumped back from the panel, said 'Not again!' and went over the side. Randolph said it happened so fast, he couldn't tell if Evans fell or jumped."

"Did Evans and Randolph have any history, any problems with each other?" Burton asked.

Radley shook her head. "In fact, Randolph was Don Evans's apprentice. They were good friends. I asked Randolph to wait in the contractor's office. Let's go see what else he has to say."

Kevin Randolph absently sipped at a cup of water, his eyes not quite focused on anything. "We wanted to get that panel done before break, so we were working faster than we should have," he said, shaking his head slowly. "We would have gotten started earlier, but Baxter needed to use Don's cell phone."

"Who is Baxter?" Radley asked, her pen ready.

"Jordan Baxter, he's an electrician, too. He has a cell phone, but the reception stinks up there, and he didn't want to walk all the way back down here. He always complains about the way Don's phone rings; it's the theme from that *Yeah, Baby!* movie. So Don gave him a hard time about using a phone that he gripes about all the time. We could have gotten started on that panel ten minutes sooner if Baxter hadn't used Don's phone."

"You heard Mr. Evans say 'Not again' before he fell," Radley said. "Any idea what that meant?"

"He probably got shocked again. But I didn't hear anything or smell any burn," Randolph said.

" 'Shocked again'?" Radley repeated. "Mr. Evans had been shocked before?"

"Oh yeah," Randolph said. "One time really bad. Put him in the hospital for a couple days. You can't do this for twenty years and not get burned a few times. I've been hit four times already, and it's only my third year."

"You might want to look into plumbing," Burton said. Randolph cracked a smile, his first since the interview started.

"Thank you for your time, Mr. Randolph. If you could

wait here a bit longer, we're going to tend to Mr. Evans," Radley said, shaking Randolph's hand.

Two floors up, Burton and Radley took pictures and videos of Evans's body, including his tools, which were scattered as far as twenty feet. Burton saw the top of a cell phone poking out of a pocket on Evans's right leg. As he leaned in for a photo, the phone buzzed to life, startling the CSI.

"Do you not hear what I don't hear?" Burton asked Radley.

"I don't hear the *Yeah, Baby!* theme, if that's what you mean. Why would he set his phone to vibrate if he enjoyed how much the ring annoyed Baxter?" she wondered.

Burton extracted the phone from the pocket with gloved hands and waited until the caller hung up or was sent to voice mail. He hoped it was a telemarketer; Mr. Evans had just made it onto the ultimate do-not-call list.

He opened the phone's flip face and scrolled through the recent calls. There was one call at 8:46 A.M., approximately the time Evans had fallen.

"Let's go downstairs," Burton said. "I have a quick call to make."

Standing out of earshot of the electricians, Burton redialed the number of the 8:46 phone call. One of the men looked at his phone and answered.

"Hello?"

"Jordan Baxter?"

"Yes?"

"This is CSI Wes Burton. You're under arrest for

murder. Would you be interested in one free phone call and a terrible lawyer?"

How did he know?

Burton's File

Jordan Baxter borrowed Don Evans's phone before Evans fell. Annoyed with the ring and angry with Evans for teasing him, Baxter switched the phone to the vibrate setting before returning it to Evans. As Kevin Randolph said, every electrician gets shocked, and Baxter knew that a bad shock begins with a vibrating sensation. Don Evans had been shocked badly before. When Baxter called him at 8:46, knowing he was working with dangerous levels of electricity, Evans thought he was getting shocked again when he felt the phone vibrate. He jumped away from the panel, falling to his death.

Did the Boa Cause the DOA?

The apartment smelled like cheese, beer, and cheap cologne, and Burton immediately knew who lived there.

"College students," he said to Detective Gibson.

"That's right," Gibson said. "We have Dennis Fuller, the deceased, in his bedroom. The other guy that lives here, Wayne Collins, found him on the floor. Looks to me like he's been asphyxiated."

"Choked on something, or strangled?" Burton asked.

"Snake," said Gibson.

"Beg your pardon?"

"Collins said that Fuller's own snake killed him. It's a boa constrictor," Gibson said. Burton thought he saw the big man shiver.

"Did the boa kill him?" Burton asked.

"If I knew that, why would you be here?" Gibson said.

"Frank," Burton said. "Are you saying that you admire me?"

"Like I admire taxes," said Gibson. "They're necessary, but I don't have to enjoy them."

"That's sweet," said Burton. "What did Collins have to say?"

Gibson flipped open his notebook. "Collins says he got home about an hour ago, watched some TV, and went to take a shower. He couldn't find his towel, and since Fuller was always taking the towel because he never washed his own, Collins went into Fuller's room to look for it. He found Fuller on the floor and called 911." Gibson closed the notebook and looked at Burton expectantly, like he was waiting for him to solve the scene right then.

"I might need to look at the body," Burton said.

"Whatever, be my guest," said Gibson. "I'll be out here."

Burton took his CRIME SEEN? tape out of vest pocket 2 and rolled it across the apartment doorway, then went into the bedroom. Fuller was sprawled facedown in the middle of the room. The clutter of CDs, incense burners, and dirty clothes on the floor would make it difficult to determine which items were evidence. Burton was not looking forward to bagging everything as he snapped photos and took video of the scene. When he was finished, Gibson leaned in the doorway, his eyes checking every corner three times.

"Frank," Burton said. "Where is the boa constrictor right now?"

"Yeah, that. We're not real sure where it is. I'll be outside," Gibson said.

"Hold on," Burton said. "I need help rolling him over." Gibson took another five looks around the room, then stepped in like it was a minefield. He hurried over to Burton, and together they rolled Fuller onto his back.

"OK, see ya," Gibson said.

"Wait," said Burton, barely hiding his smile. He looked into Fuller's eyes and saw small red dots in the white areas. "He has petechial hemorrhaging, so strangulation was probably the cause of death."

"Yeah, we knew that. Bye-bye," Gibson tried again.

"But look at this," Burton said, pointing to Fuller's throat. "He has a pattern imprinted on his neck. It looks like a spiral, and it goes across the front and sides, but not the back. I don't see any abrasions, so it was made by something soft."

"Like slimy snake scales?" Gibson said, his voice getting high.

"Snakes aren't slimy," Burton said. "But murdering roommates are. We need to find that towel."

Why did Burton want the towel?

Burton's File

Boa constrictors do kill their prey by suffocation, but they wrap themselves around the chest of their victim and tighten with each breath, making it impossible for the prey to inhale. The throat does not expand and contract while a person is breathing, so the snake would not choose to wrap itself around that area of the body. The imprints on Fuller's throat did not continue to the back of his neck; if the snake had choked him, the imprint would have wound all the way around his neck, allowing the boa to squeeze. Those imprints, combined with the spiral marks in them, indicate that Fuller was strangled from behind by a twisted piece of soft fabric. Perhaps a dirty bath towel?

Bringing the Truth to Light

"Boy, this guy's a worse driver than my wife," Detective Gibson said, standing next to the wrecked truck on the side of the road. "And she's half blind."

"That explains why she married you," said Burton as he tied off the end of his CRIME SCENE — DO NOT CROSS / CRIME SEEN? STICK AROUND tape. Mike Trellis coughed to hide his smile. It was nearly 9:00 P.M. and the sky was dark, but the portable lights and road flares bathed the scene as if it were day.

"Why don't you crawl under the front tire real quick, Burton," Gibson said. "I want to check something."

"What?" Burton asked, peering around the tire in question.

"How long you can live with the front tire on top of you," Gibson replied.

"Aw, there's that police brotherhood thing I've been hearing about," Trellis said. "It brings a tear to my eye."

"All right, boys," Burton said. "Let's get down to business. Gibson, do you have the driver's statement?"

Gibson flipped open his notepad. "The driver, Glenn Ward, was driving down St. Joseph Avenue, the road we are currently standing on, around 8:00 P.M. He didn't have his headlights on and didn't see the joggers until it was too late. His vehicle struck all four joggers, killing two of them, putting one in critical condition. They all had reflective vests on, but it didn't matter since his lights were off. They're at Lakeview Hospital right now. Ward got a sprained ankle and a bloody nose, treated and released by the EMTs. He's in the back of that squad car right now." Gibson pointed to a police car across the road, about fifty yards away. "He's pretty upset over the whole thing, and he keeps saying 'I told them, I told them.'"

"Told who what?" Burton asked.

"Let's go see," Gibson said and headed for the squad car.

"Mr. Ward, this is Wes Burton, he's a crime scene investigator," said Gibson. Ward looked up from the passenger seat. He held a bloody paper towel under his nose.

"Hello," he said, and checked the towel for fresh blood. Apparently satisfied, he let his hands fall into his lap.

"Earlier you were saying 'I told them.' Can you explain what that meant?" Gibson asked.

"Yeah," Ward said. "I see those joggers just about every night on my way home from work, and the other day I pulled over and talked to them. They run in the road, all spread out alongside each other, instead of single file on the sidewalk like they should. I told them that I had to swerve into oncoming traffic to avoid them, and it made me nervous."

"And tonight you just didn't see them?" Gibson said.

"Right," said Ward. "I didn't think it was dark enough for my headlights. I guess they didn't see me coming, and I sure didn't see them. They shouldn't have been in the road like that anyway, right?"

"Thanks, Mr. Ward," Burton said. "Just wait here,

please." Burton and Gibson walked back to the truck, where Trellis was shining a flashlight into the broken right headlight.

"Check it out, boss," he said. Burton took the flashlight and peered into the broken headlight. After a few moments, he took his portable inspection microscope out of vest pocket 20 and focused it through the jagged glass. The small tool could magnify items from eighteen up to thirty-six times.

"What are you looking at?" Gibson said.

"The wire inside the headlight," said Burton, still peering through his mini microscope.

"You mean the filament?" Gibson said, and Burton looked at him with raised eyebrows.

"Well, yes," he said, "but I didn't think you'd know what that word meant."

"Please," said Gibson. "I do all the work on my Chevys myself. I can swap out a starter and change the oil in the time it takes Trellis here to comb his hair."

Trellis touched his head. "Is my hair okay?"

Gibson ignored him. "Why are you looking at the filament?" he said to Burton.

"As you know," Burton said, thinking he'd never say those words to Gibson, "the filament in a headlight is a thin wire encased in a tube of glass. When electricity is passed through the wire, it becomes extremely hot and creates a bright beam of light."

"I'm still with you," Gibson said.

"When Ward hit the joggers," said Burton, "it broke the tube of glass around the filament, but the filament stayed intact. Take a close look at the filament and tell me what you see."

Trellis stepped forward, and Burton held his hand up. "I was talking to Gibson," he said. The technician's mouth opened then closed. Gibson smiled at him then examined the filament through the mini microscope.

"I see little beads of glass on the filament," Gibson said. "But I gotta tell you, I don't know what significance that has."

Trellis finally got his mouth to work. "Maybe if I had a look, it would jog my memory. Get it? Because they were jogging."

"I changed my mind," Gibson said. "I want *you* to get under the tire instead of Burton." He turned to the head CSI. "So what is it about the filament? What did you see?"

"I saw evidence that needs some running shoes of its own, because it'll be standing up in court," Burton said. "Ward saw the joggers coming, and he hit them on purpose."

How did he know?

Burton's File

When the headlight broke, pieces of glass came in contact with the filament and melted, forming the beads. For this to happen, the filament had to have been extremely hot, indicating that Ward had his headlights on when he hit the joggers.

Dental Breakdown

Burton and Detective Gibson stood next to the hospital bed and looked down at Rick Willard, who was in a coma. Willard's entire body was swollen, but his legs, ankles, and feet were especially puffy. Bruises covered most of his arms, and there were a few splotches on his face and neck where it looked like he'd taken a few punches.

"He's got it right," Burton said. "If you have to be in a hospital, you're best off being in a coma. That way, you don't even know you're there." Burton didn't like hospitals one bit.

"Maybe he does know," Gibson said. "I mean, the poor guy's in a coma from his kidneys failing after he takes a beating, and you're here talking about how lucky he is. I think he'd rather be awake and watching bad daytime TV and eating junk food. Maybe he can hear you right now, and he's adding you to the list of people he's going to chase when he wakes up." He looked at Willard. "Mr. Willard, this is Detective Gibson. I think you look great, and I hope you get better real soon." He smiled at Burton, happy that he wasn't on Willard's hit list.

"Can I take my samples and go?" Burton asked.

"Who's stopping you?" Gibson said, stepping back from the bed. Burton gently lifted Willard's left hand and looked at the fingernails. There was nothing there. He did the same with the right hand and again found nothing.

"There's no trace evidence under the fingernails," Burton said. "I don't think he put up much of a fight when he was attacked."

"There wasn't any sign of a struggle at his apartment," Gibson said. "I talked to the guy who lives next door, and he didn't hear anything that sounded like a fight. It's possible that whoever did this beat him up somewhere else, and he made it home before passing out. And I tell you, for a dentist, it wasn't that nice of a place."

"Willard is a dentist?" said Burton, opening his pad to take down the new information.

"I assume so," Gibson said. "His apartment had that smell."

"What smell?" Burton didn't start writing yet.

"You know, that dentist smell. They all have it."

"Do you mean dentists' offices have the smell, or the dentists do?" Burton asked.

"What?"

"Did you smell something in his apartment that reminded you of a dentist's office," Burton said slowly, "or of your dentist in particular?"

Gibson considered for a moment. "The dentist's office," he finally decided. "I don't know what my dentist smells like."

Burton ignored him and lifted the medical chart off the foot of the bed. He glanced down the face sheet until he came to the line "Occupation."

"Willard is unemployed," he said.

"Oh," said Gibson. "Then I guess his apartment was pretty nice."

"This chart shows that he has very limited medical insurance and no dental insurance," Burton said. "So he wouldn't have even been in a dentist's office as a patient, let alone a doctor. So where did that smell come from?"

"Not from me," Gibson said. "I had chili for lunch. If it came from me, it wouldn't smell like a dentist's."

Burton flipped through the chart some more. "The doctor checked his mouth for broken or missing teeth and found extreme swelling and inflammation along the upper gum line, but it had been there for a few days, so it wasn't a result of the fight. So Willard had a toothache but couldn't go to the dentist."

"So he had a dentist come to him?" Gibson offered. "And when he couldn't pay, the dentist beat him up? We've got a slimy, vicious dentist on the loose!"

"I don't think so," Burton said. "The culprit we're looking for is oily, and it's still in Willard's apartment."

How did he know?

Burton's File

Willard had a terrible toothache and used clove oil to soothe the pain. Eugenol, the active ingredient in clove oil, was the source of the "dentist smell." It's used as a pain reliever by dental professionals and is in most over-the-counter toothache medicines. What Willard didn't know is that an overdose of clove oil can cause kidney failure, which can result in swelling, bruising, and eventually, coma.

Donut Assume

Burton parked his truck and walked toward the small donut shop. What was left of it, anyway.

"Watch the glass," Detective Radley said from inside the burnt-out building. The sidewalk and street beyond it were peppered with shards of glass, which flew as far as forty feet when the donut shop exploded.

"Good thing this happened at night, when no one was around," Burton said. "We'd have some people puzzles to put back together."

Mike Trellis was collecting sample materials from inside the shop and placing them in sealed glass jars. He was working quickly, because if the explosion was the result of arson and the criminal used a petroleum-based accelerant such as gasoline, the trace vapors would soon evaporate.

"Can you imagine the bad jokes we're going to hear about this?" Trellis asked. "People will say that the cops will solve this one in a hurry, since it was a donut shop."

"I don't buy donuts," Burton said. "I'm a muffin guy."

"Really?" Trellis stopped his collection process and looked suspiciously at Burton. "How come?"

"You get more for your money with a muffin," Burton said. "A donut comes with a hole in it. It's a matter of economics, really."

Radley nodded at this, seeing the logic.

"What about donuts with filling?" Trellis asked,

sounding like he hoped he'd ruined Burton's theory with one question.

"Those are for suckers," Burton replied, and Trellis sagged. "It's like they're saying, 'We know we're ripping you off by having a hole in the middle, so here's some jam to keep you quiet.' No thanks. Not for me."

"Interesting," Radley said, more to herself than the two crime scene investigators. "I wonder if a person's choice of breakfast pastry is an indicator of any other behavior in his or her life. . . . Maybe this could be a sub-chapter in my book."

"But I've seen you eat donuts before," Trellis said, a look of complete confusion on his face.

"Oh, I'll *eat* donuts," Burton said. "I just won't buy them."

Trellis shook his head. "I think your donut theory has a few holes in it," he said. "Get it? Because of —"

"Yeah, I get it," Burton interrupted. Then he asked, "What do you think happened here?"

"From the spread of the glass and destruction of the kitchen in back," Trellis said, resuming his sample taking, "it was definitely an explosion. Whether it was gas or placed explosives, I'm not sure yet. I've found a few melted kitchen timers that could have been used as part of an explosive device, but it's a donut shop, so they might just be regular old-timers."

"Is the owner looking at a big insurance payoff after this?" Burton asked Radley.

"He is insured, but it's not a huge amount by any means," she said. "And he's not struggling, either. This shop does very well during the week, and there's a line out the door most weekends."

"He makes a great New York cheesecake donut," Trellis said, then gave Burton a flat look. "Not that you'd know."

Burton rolled his eyes at Radley. "I'll check out back," he said. "See if there are any tire marks from someone making a quick getaway."

Behind the donut shop, Burton found stacks of plastic crates, a trash bin, a recycling bin, and several parking spots — but no fresh tire marks. He checked the rear security door to the shop and saw no signs of forced entry, then he headed for the trash bin. He was constantly amazed at what criminals threw away, as if the garbage can were some portal to another dimension instead of a handy holding tank for clues.

Burton took one look in the trash bin, smiled, and went to get Radley and Trellis. When he brought them back, they didn't share his happiness.

"Eggs?" Radley said. "Why would he throw out dozens of eggs?"

Trellis leaned into the bin and inhaled deeply. Radley shuddered. "They don't smell rotten," he said.

"They aren't," Burton said. "But the donut maker thought they were. You can dunk the arson investigation. This was an accident."

How did Burton know?

Burton's File

Natural gas, which is used for cooking and heating, is invisible and odorless. In order for us to detect possible leaks, Mercaptan, which contains sulfur, is added to the gas. If you've ever smelled sulfur before, you won't forget it. It smells like rotten eggs.

The natural gas leak in the donut bakery made the chef think his eggs were rotten, so he threw them away.

Exit, Stage Death

"This is Rufus Weatherton, the stage manager here at the Civic Theater," Detective Radley said, introducing Burton and Mike Trellis.

"Quite pleased to make your acquaintance," Weatherton said, his English accent sounding very impressive. The four of them stood on the theater's stage, near the front. They were careful to stay out of the crime scene, near center stage, in the middle of scenery that hadn't been touched since the night before.

"Likewise," said Burton. "Although you're probably wishing that we could meet under different circumstances."

"Dreadful situation, isn't it?" Weatherton said. "As far as I know, the Civic has never before had an actor die in the middle of a performance. And on opening night! We've had a few stagehands pass on during shows, the drunken sots. They fall from the catwalks like they get paid extra to do so!"

"Maybe they should call them 'can't walks' instead," Trellis offered. "Get it? Because they're hard to walk on." Weatherton looked at Trellis as though he were a Martian. Burton coughed.

"So," Radley said to Weatherton as she shot Trellis a harsh look. "The performer's name was Shelly Victoria, and she died of unknown causes during Act Two, is that correct?"

"Indeed," Weatherton said. "It was during the only

dance number in the production, Miss Victoria's tap routine. The director added it in at the last moment, though none of us could understand why."

"Did the director and Victoria have any trouble?" Radley asked.

"Oh, they despised one another," Weatherton said huffily. "They used to be a lovey couple before the production, but there were some arguments during rehearsals, and eventually they could barely stand to be in the same room. Even when the room's this big." He gestured toward the theater's cathedral ceiling.

"And she just dropped to the stage?" Burton asked.

"I'm afraid so," said Weatherton. "My guess would be a heart attack or stroke, except she was so young."

"Her medical records didn't show a history of heart trouble or high cholesterol," Burton said. "But rest assured, our forensic pathologist, Dr. Crown, will be able to determine the cause of death," Burton said. "But while we wait, let's see if we can figure it out ourselves. Thanks for your time, Mr. Weatherton."

"If you need anything at all," Weatherton said with a small bow, "I'll be right over here." He walked offstage, where he checked his hair in a mirror.

"Did he go stage left or stage right?" Trellis asked. "I can never remember."

"It's your left and right as you stand onstage and face the audience," Burton said, turning to look at the empty seats.

"Does the audience call it 'audience left'?" Trellis asked.

"Mike — check the crime scene," Burton said. Once he was busy, Radley leaned toward Burton.

"This is a tremendous opportunity," she said in a low voice.

"You want to get into acting?" Burton asked, surprised.

"No, for my book," said Radley. "Criminals are liars, and who knows more about lying than an actor? They're professional liars! I could get some great insight into motivation, techniques for altering one's personality, and —"

Radley stopped short when she saw Weatherton standing next to her. She hoped he hadn't heard the part about professional liars. He had. Weatherton looked around to make sure no one else was within earshot before he spoke.

"It's true, in the theater, we lie," Weatherton said, and the twangy Southern accent that came out of his mouth made Burton do a double take.

"My name isn't Weatherton, it's Boyd," he said. "I figure y'all should hear it from me instead of someone else, or it might seem like I'm hiding my identity."

"Thanks, Mr. Boyd," Radley said, still thrown off by the accent. "Is there anything else we should know?"

"Not about me," Boyd said. "Except that I didn't kill Victoria. She was a stage manager's dream. We had the first week sold out before opening night because of her. She worked hard and never complained. Except about the director, of course. She wanted to have him fired from day one. I think he put that dance number in the show just to get back at her. Can you imagine? Making the leading lady tap-dance in a puddle! In a scene that takes place in the desert!"

"Thanks again, Mr. Boyd," Burton said, and left him with Radley. He headed over to Trellis, who was following an extension cord from backstage, through the scenery, to where it ended at center stage.

"What did you find?" Burton asked.

"This cord is plugged in over there, runs hidden through the set, and ends here," Trellis said. "But there's no plug on this end. It's just frayed wires."

"Detective Radley," Burton called. "We need to send some officers to arrest the director. I want to talk to him about his electrifying opening night."

How did Victoria die?

Burton's File

The director was upset about his breakup with Shelly Victoria and wanted to end her career — for good. He put in the last-minute scene that had her tap-dance in a puddle, then added a prop of his own — the frayed extension cord. When she stepped into the puddle, the electricity from the cord flowed into the metal taps on her shoes, electrocuting Victoria.

First-Degree Birder

Ed leaped over logs and scuttled under branches, hot on the trail, her orange vest jingling with every step. Burton followed, not quite out of breath but wishing he had Ed's stamina. They were in the state park forest, with hundreds of square miles of woods, valleys, hills, and fields to search.

"Good girl, Ed, keep going," Burton said. Almost before he could finish the sentence, Ed bounded back toward him and sat down, her ears up and her body leaning ahead, anxious to lead Burton to the source of the scent.

"What did you find? Show me!" Burton said, breaking into a sprint. Ed took off, leading Burton to a stand of pine trees that formed a canopy. Ed disappeared into the spiny branches, and Burton heard a voice say "Good girl! What a smarty!"

Ed emerged from the trees, followed by Mike Trellis, the subject of the search. He and Burton were working Ed through some search-and-rescue drills to keep her sharp and happy. She was a working dog and didn't enjoy unemployment.

"Good job, Exhibit D!" Burton said and tossed her a tennis ball. The ball was Ed's reward for a job well done, and she had been expecting the throw with wide eyes and a blurred tail.

"Did she have any trouble finding me?" Trellis asked, brushing pine needles off his clothes.

"Not really," Burton said. "A few hitches when she found some raccoon poop, but no big problems. It probably helped that you had burritos for dinner last night. She probably thought she was tracking a septic tank."

"Help!"

Trellis closed his mouth before he could respond to Burton's jab. "Did you hear that?" he asked instead.

"Sounded like 'help,'" Burton answered, his head tilted to the side.

"Someone help!" The voice sounded close by, but Burton knew the acoustics in this kind of terrain were tricky. He could tell which direction it was coming from, though, and he and Trellis started that way.

"Come on, Ed," Burton said. "Bring your ball." Ed trotted along with the two men, her ball held loosely in her mouth. The three of them traveled for about ten minutes, using a call-and-response system with the voice to home in on the caller's location. Finally, they came to a small clearing, where a man stood over a figure lying faceup in the dirt.

"Thank goodness!" the man said, his voice hoarse from all the yelling. "I think this guy might be in trouble. I don't think he's breathing!"

Trellis knelt by the prone man and listened for breathing, then checked for a pulse. Nothing. When his fingers left the man's throat, the white spots caused by their pressure quickly returned to the man's normal skin tone.

"I'm going to initiate CPR," Trellis said and opened the man's vest, which had the *Field Guide to North American*

Birds sticking out of a front pocket. Poking out from another pouch was a tattered notebook, and a small pair of binoculars lay on the ground next to the man's foot.

Once he was sure Trellis didn't need assistance, Burton looked at the man who called for help, who was now sitting on a log with his head in his hands. He noticed a similar spotting scope around his neck and a patch on his vest that said THE KIRTLAND'S WARBLER CLUB — MEMBERSHIP: 1.

"Are you two bird-watchers?" Burton asked.

"Birders," the man said without looking up.

"Birders?" said Burton. "So you bird?"

"That's right. What's the problem?"

"Well," Burton said. "Runners run, climbers climb, so birders . . . bird?"

"No, we spot birds and record the sightings," the man said, finally looking at Burton. "Who are you, anyway? I've been yelling for over an hour."

"I'm Wes Burton, CSI, and this is Mike Trellis, my technician. That's Ed, my dog. And your name is?"

"Eagle Eye Dorchester," the man said. Burton looked at him. "Thomas Dorchester," he said after a moment.

"Okay, Thomas," Burton said. "What happened here?"

"I was in a great spot," Dorchester said, "trying to attract a black-backed woodpecker, when I heard this yelp and a crash, like branches breaking. I ran over here to see what happened and found him like this. I didn't even know he was out here until then. I think he fell out of a tree."

Burton looked at Trellis, who had given up on the CPR and was checking for signs of trauma. "There's blood on the back of his head," Trellis said. "Could be a fractured skull, caused by a blow to the head. Or a fall, I guess."

"Do you know this man's name?" Burton asked Dorchester.

"No, I've never seen him out here before," he said.

Burton slipped on a latex glove from vest pocket 5 and eased the tattered notebook out of the man's pouch. He flipped through the pages, hoping to find an *If found, please return to So-and-So* notice. The pages were filled with sketches and scribblings of birds spotted, and the entry on the last written page caught Burton's eye. It was written in large block letters, surrounded by exclamation points: "THE KIRTLAND'S WARBLER! Perched on branch and singing!"

"That's a pretty exclusive club you're in," Burton said, pointing to Dorchester's patch. "Did you know that everyone in it is a murderer?"

How did Burton know?

Burton's File

Dorchester said that he'd been yelling for help for over an hour, but when Trellis checked the body for a pulse, his fingers made white marks on the tissue. When he removed the pressure, blood flowed back into the tissue, returning it to its normal color. This is called blanching and only occurs when a body has been dead for less than thirty minutes. When Trellis, Ed, and I came upon the scene, the man had been dead for less than half an hour, proving Dorchester a liar.

Dorchester didn't want anyone else in his exclusive birder club, so he used another kind of club on the man's head to keep it that way.

Her Son and Arson

Detective Gibson set the cup of coffee down on the interview table for Donald Hawes, who sipped it immediately and often.

"I'm not exactly sure why I'm here," Hawes said. "I have a lot of things to attend to, you know. My mother's funeral, for one, and —" He broke down, the tears coming again, followed by the sobbing. Gibson rolled his eyes and moved the box of tissues closer.

"That's pretty much why you are here," Burton said. "We wanted to make sure you didn't have anything to tell us before your mother is buried."

"Like what?" Hawes said, honking into a tissue. "That I'm a terrible son for getting out of a burning house while my mother got left inside? Okay, I'll say it."

"You just did," Gibson said. "We don't need a rerun."

"You said that the fire started in the hallway outside her room," Burton said. "So you couldn't get in to help her out."

"That's right," Hawes said miserably. "There was nothing I could do."

"You mother was bedridden, is that right?" Gibson asked.

"Yes," Hawes said. "She was very ill. It may have been a mercy for her to pass on, you know."

"Oh, I know," Gibson muttered. "So while she was laid

up in bed for the past few months, you were nice enough to cash her Social Security and pension checks. We have the slips from the bank, and the checks, signed by you. The last one is dated December tenth, one week ago."

"We went through the proper channels for that," Hawes said, his voice still heavy with grief. "I had to pay for her medication somehow."

"What was she taking?" Burton asked. "It may be conclusive during the autopsy."

"What autopsy?" Hawes said, his voice climbing. "I didn't approve that!"

"We're grown-ups, we don't need your permission," Gibson snarled. "What was she taking?"

"Um, cyclosporine," Hawes said. "For her arthritis."

"All right, Mr. Hawes," Burton said. "Please stay here with Detective Gibson. I need to check a few things in the lab, then we'll talk some more."

Burton left the two men in the interview room and headed for the lab, where Mike Trellis was waiting for him. He had just returned from the Hawes house and was covered from head to toe with ashes and soot.

"What do you see?" Trellis asked, and handed Burton a photo of Mrs. Hawes's bedroom. "This was taken from the hall doorway."

"I see a guy who needs a shower and a Laundromat," Burton said. "And maybe a few hours at the gym."

"Not me, the photo," Trellis said, and touched his mid-section. "The gym, really?"

"I see a charred body, lying supine on a burned bed, on the other side of the room," Burton said. "I see a V-shaped burn going from the bed, up the wall, and onto the ceiling."

"Exactly," Trellis said. "See how the arms and legs are straight?"

"Indeed I do," said Burton. "What about the prescription?"

"Cyclosporine," Trellis said, referring to his notes. "One pill a day, same time every day. She had a thirty-pill prescription, and it was last filled on October thirteenth."

"So if he cashed her last check in December," Burton said, "but hasn't filled her prescription in almost two months . . ."

"Someone hasn't been taking her pills," Trellis said. "Or — maybe she hasn't needed them."

"Nice work, Mike," Burton said. "Now about that shower . . ."

"I thought I'd do some sit-ups in your office first," Trellis said, flakes of ash falling off him with every move. "You know, because of my weight problem and all."

"I take it back," Burton said over his shoulder as he headed back to the interview room. .

"Detective Gibson won't get me any more tissues," Hawes said when Burton opened the door.

"Can't you just use imaginary ones?" Burton asked. "You know, fake tissues for fake tears?"

"What are you implying?" Hawes asked in a how-dare-you tone.

"I'm not implying anything," Burton said. "I'm telling, and I'm proving. You mother has been dead for over a month, and the fire started in her bed."

How did Burton know?

Burton's File

When a body burns, the heat from the fire dehydrates the body's muscles and causes them to contract into what is known as the "boxer's posture." Legs and arms bend, and the fists tuck beneath the chin. Mrs. Hawes was lying flat on her bed, which meant that her body was already completely dehydrated before the fire started, since only death can cause that much dehydration.

Fire tends to rise and spread from its point of origin. If the flames had entered the room from the hall, they would have converged on Mrs. Hawes and her bed, which were on the other side of the room. The V-shaped burn on her bedroom wall points down to her bed, indicating that's where the flame started, not finished.

Donald was cashing her checks but not filling her prescriptions, and he decided to get rid of the evidence by faking her death in a fire.

If the Clue Fits

Burton surveyed the living-room floor again, tilting his head this way and that to try to get a better angle. The footprints on the orange carpet told the story of what happened, but so far the tale was confusing.

"Tilt it down a little," Burton said to Trellis, who aimed the work light slightly lower. Burton studied the carpet once more, then stood up. The prints showed that someone wearing size 9 tennis shoes had walked from place to place around the room, followed by someone wearing size 12 work boots. The prints went throughout the house, but this carpet had retained the best samples.

"Let's get photos of all these prints," Burton told Trellis. "I want a left and right comparison of the smaller shoeprints, and the same for the bigger bootprints. Make sure you take the photos from directly above the print; I don't want any distortions."

"You know what's distorted?" Trellis asked. "This carpet. Who picks out orange carpet? Someone who drops a lot of pumpkins and doesn't want the stains to show?"

"Thank you, Mike," Burton said, and walked outside. Radley was taking a statement from the victim, Barry Anderson, who looked at Burton as he approached.

"Do you think you'll catch him?" Anderson asked. "He took all the jewelry, the DVD player, my work laptop, the —"

"I've got it all in the report, Mr. Anderson," Radley said.

"We'll do to everything we can to locate the burglar and your belongings."

"Burglar?" Anderson cried. "What about kidnapper? He grabbed me in the driveway and made me take him inside! Then he followed me around the house while I loaded all my things into my best suitcase for him! He finally left when I couldn't fit anything else in it. It got so heavy, I could barely carry it around. Can I press charges for assault, too? My shoulder's killing me!" Anderson displayed his pain by rotating his right arm at the shoulder, rubbing the area with his left hand.

"Would you like medical attention?" Radley asked.

"I think that might be for the best," Anderson said, suddenly looking very weak.

"Why don't you sit down, put your feet up?" Burton suggested. "I need to get a sample of your shoeprint, anyway, for comparison."

"Sure, whatever you need," Anderson said, and sat down on the front steps. He took off his tennis shoes, which Burton saw were size 9. He took them inside, where Trellis was transferring the footprint images to his laptop.

"We can develop these photos when we get back to the lab," Trellis said. "But if you want a quick look at the best samples, I flagged them."

"Show me," Burton said. Trellis carefully made his way toward the middle of the room, careful not to disturb the path of evidence.

"See here?" he asked Burton. "The shoeprints are

equally deep, but the bootprints show the right print is deeper than the left. That pattern is consistent throughout the house but, like I said, this is the best example of it."

From Trellis's tone of voice, Burton knew there was more. "What else do you have?" he said.

"How nice of you to ask," Trellis said. "Walk this way." He stepped up onto the couch and walked across it to the other end, then peered over the back. Burton followed.

"Here we have the elusive *bootus printus*," Trellis whispered in a horrible Australian accent. "What a beauty she is! Notice how the print is clear from the heel to the ball of the foot, but in the toe area it gets lighter? Like the toes weren't pressed into the carpet?"

"I see it," Burton said. "Is that consistent for the rest of the prints, too?"

"Righto, mate," Trellis said, the accent still there.

"That's the worst impression I've ever heard," Burton said. "Maybe you ought to look into mime school."

Outside, Radley was watching while a pair of EMTs looked Anderson over, squeezing his shoulder and apologizing when he yelped in pain.

"What do you think?" Radley asked as Burton returned.

"I think we need to put some handcuffs on Anderson, whether his shoulder hurts or not," Burton said.

How did Burton know?

Burton's File

Anderson, who was wearing the size 9 shoes, said he was forced to carry his suitcase around the house and fill it with items while the thief followed him. He also claimed this task injured his right shoulder. However, the footprints in the carpet indicated that the person wearing the boots did the heavy lifting with his right hand, since the right boot prints were deeper than the left.

Trellis also pointed out that the boot prints were well formed from the heel to the ball of the foot, but the toe left a very light impression. This indicates that someone was wearing boots that were too big for his feet, with the toe area of the boot having nothing in it. Anderson walked around his house in his shoes, then changed to bigger boots and retraced his steps, loading up on "stolen" items. We'll see how well he can fill the shoes of someone who tried to commit insurance fraud.

Sparking a Controversy

"Is that the security camera's tape from the robbery?" Burton asked Mike Trellis. Trellis was sitting in front of a television in the crime lab, leaning dangerously close to the screen. Burton stood next to him and watched the crime replay in black and white.

"Okay," Trellis said. "Here he is coming into the convenience store with a mask on. He pulls a revolver out of his belt and points it at the guy behind the counter and says 'Gimme all the money.' Now he's stuffing the money in his left-side jacket pocket with his free hand. Now he tells the clerk to get down and not to call the cops. The clerk gets down. He eventually does call the cops, though."

"Thanks for ruining the ending," Burton said.

"My pleasure," said Trellis, who went back to narrating the video. "The robber leaves, and we switch to camera two, which is outside the front door and shows the parking lot. The robber runs into the lot, sees this guy here walking toward him, and he fires. We don't know if he was aiming at the guy or not, but the bullet hits the pavement about ten feet away from the walker."

Trellis froze the tape and rewound it, then played it back in slow motion. Burton could see the gun fire, and he saw the sparks that flew off the parking lot where the bullet struck. "Did you recover the bullet?"

"No," Trellis said. "The sparks there are a ricochet. Even if we did find the slug, we wouldn't be able to match it to anything. Too mangled."

"What happens next?" Burton asked. Trellis continued the playback.

"After he fires the shot, the robber runs off to the right and around the corner of the store, where he's between cameras for two and a half seconds. Now, while he's invisible, you can see the guy he shot at flinch again, like he's still being shot at. But the gun only has one empty shell, and the robber didn't have time to reload, so it could be that the guy was confused and only heard one shot but thought he heard two. Then we pick up the robber with camera three, which is around the corner and shows the alley between the convenience store and the building next to it. Here, we see him run down the alley and dump the gun in the trash receptacle, where I recovered it. I can show you the footage of me, if you like. It's an award-winning performance."

"Which award?" Burton said. "Most Likely to Smell Like Garbage for the Rest of the Day?" Trellis sniffed his shirt and frowned. "Where's the gun?" asked Burton.

"I put it on the worktable, over there," Trellis said and pointed. "The serial number has been ground away. I was hoping you could work your magnetic magic on it."

Burton found the revolver in a plastic evidence bag. The metal had fingerprint dust on it, and he could see several prints and partial prints raised by the dust.

"Did you get a match on any of these prints?" he asked.

"Not yet," said Trellis. "I'm running them through the software right now, but, like you say, 'Evidence needs more than one shoe to stand up in court. Unless it's a really big shoe that both feet can fit in.'"

"I don't think I say that," Burton said as he took the revolver out of the plastic bag. "Do you want to watch and learn over here?" Trellis stopped the tape and walked over, rubbing his eyes. "Okay," Burton said, doing some narration of his own while he worked. "When the serial number gets stamped into the gun, it changes the magnetic properties of the metal around the serial number. Even if someone grinds the serial number off, the metal is still distorted from the stamping process. If we magnetize the gun, the magnetic forces will act differently around the altered metal. Then we dust the serial number area with metal powder, which collects in the altered metal and reveals the serial number."

Burton stepped back and let Trellis have a look. He saw the serial number there, written in magnetized metal shavings. "Amazing," Trellis said. "See, this is the kind of stuff that attracted me to this line of work." He looked at Burton, who just looked back.

"Get it?" Trellis asked. "Because it's a magnet, it attracted me to this job."

"Where are the bullets for this gun?" Burton asked. Trellis stepped back.

"Okay, I admit it," he said. "That was a pretty bad joke, but you don't have to shoot me."

"If I was going to shoot you over a bad joke," Burton said, "you'd look like Swiss cheese by now. I just want to see if we can trace the bullet manufacturer."

Trellis handed him two evidence bags, one with five bullets and the other with one empty shell. As soon as Burton had the bullets, the technician hustled back to his television and spun the large TV so it was between him and Burton. He peeked over the top once, then disappeared.

Burton shook his head while he took the five bullets out of the bag. He picked one up and examined the back end, looking for manufacturer information, then spun the bullet and looked at the nose. The lead slug was dull under the bright laboratory lights. Burton looked at each bullet and saw that none of them had copper jackets on the tip; they were all lead slugs.

"Mike," he said, "we just ran the fingerprints and serial number from the wrong gun. The robber's trying to shoot us in the wrong direction."

How did Burton know?

Burton's File

In the security video from camera two, sparks flew off the pavement when the robber fired his pistol at the approaching man. The gun in the lab had lead slugs with no copper jackets. Lead by itself is too soft to create the tiny fragments that become sparks. Then the robber goes off camera, and the man in the parking lot flinches again, indicating another gunshot. That was the robber firing the second gun, with someone else's fingerprints on it. That was the gun he dumped in the trash for us to find.

Strike Three, You're Guilty!

"Vandalism?" Burton said when he and Trellis entered the small accounting office. "I think 'small nuclear explosion' is a better description." The office was in ruins, with papers, glass, desks, chairs, file cabinets, and other supplies strewn all over the floor. Just about every piece of furniture had been broken in at least one place.

"Today's Monday," Detective Radley said from the middle of the room. "Whoever broke in could have had all weekend to wreak havoc in here."

"Any suspects?" Burton asked, slipping on a pair of latex gloves from vest pocket 5.

"Yes, this is interesting," Radley said. "We have two security guards in custody, and each one of them says that the other did it. They both had access to this office, and they're both clients of the accountant. The bad part is that they both were wearing leather gloves when we detained them, so chances are slim that we'll find any fingerprints here. If you ask me, we're dealing with the topic of one of the biggest chapters in my book so far: money."

Burton nodded. "When you ask why someone committed a crime, that's a pretty popular answer."

"Money is a popular answer no matter what the question is," Trellis said. "Question: Why are you still in that lousy job? Answer: The money. Question: Why don't you move to a better apartment? Answer: Not enough money."

"I may have found something here," Radley said from across the room. "Looks like the vandal used it as a blunt object to break the furniture."

Burton and Trellis picked their way through the office and joined Radley. "A wooden bat," Burton said. He pulled a fingerprint brush out of vest pocket 16 and print powder out of 22. "Mike, take some photos and video of the bat while I get ready to dust it for prints."

"Sure thing," Trellis said and got to work. Burton and Radley waited, looking at him. He stopped taking photos and looked back at them.

"What?" he said. "Do I have something on my face?"

"We're waiting," said Radley.

"Waiting for what?" Trellis said, confused.

"We know you've got one," Burton said. "Just get on with it so we can continue."

"I don't know what you're talking —" Trellis started, then stopped. "Oh, wait. You mean one of my hilarious jokes that lighten the mood and make everyone happy?"

"That's not how I would describe them," Burton said. "But we're still waiting."

"I'm hurt, you guys," Trellis said, resuming his photography. "This is a serious crime, and you expect me to joke about it." Burton and Radley looked at each other, both of them a bit embarrassed.

Trellis shook his head. "Some perpetrator could be on the loose right now, committing foul play as we speak. Get it? Foul play? Because he used a bat."

Burton and Radley groaned but were relieved to have the most painful part of the investigation out of the way. When Trellis was done with the photography, Burton moved in with the print kit. He dusted the length of the bat, but no obvious prints showed up.

"Nothing?" Radley said over his shoulder.

"I wouldn't say that." Burton pointed to a pattern in the powder. "What does that look like to you?"

Radley tilted her head to one side, then the other. "It looks like a contact print, like the bat was pressed against someone's skin. But we can't match that to anything. It could be from anywhere, on anyone's body!"

"I'm not taking prints off a security guard's entire body," Trellis said.

"That won't be necessary," Burton said. "I don't need to see the guards. I only need their gloves."

How will Burton match the print to the vandal?

Burton's File

Even though the vandal was wearing gloves, he still left a distinctive print. Leather is animal hide, and it leaves a print just like any other skin. By matching the leather glove to the print on the bat, the vandal was easy to identify. To quote Trellis at the time of the arrest: "The guy didn't just like his bat. He gloved it."

The Corporate Corpse

The cubicles were about the same size as Burton's CSI truck, and the technical writers were packed in four to a cube. They clacked away on their keyboards, most of them wearing headphones and sipping cups of water from the cooler at the end of the office aisle. Burton peered over the top of the cubicle walls and saw that they covered the entire office floor.

"How many people work in this office?" he asked Ellen North, who was his escort. The pharmaceutical company didn't allow outsiders to wander around the plant alone, for security and confidentiality reasons.

"There are approximately three hundred employees on this floor," North said. "But in the entire building? I'd have to check."

"Does everyone in the building have access to this area?" Detective Radley asked.

"No," North said. "If they don't work on this floor or have special access, they can't get into this room."

Burton nodded, knowing that policy is one thing but reality is another. "Do you know if Mr. Bell had any arguments or conflicts with an employee recently?" Bell was currently being photographed by Mike Trellis in the bathroom where his body had been discovered two hours ago. From the state of the bathroom, Bell had obviously been nauseous along with some bowel issues, and the sudden onset of the symptoms waved a big flag at the crew that said *poison*. Trellis had guessed arsenic, and Burton thought he could be right.

"No one reported anything," North said. "But it's a time of high stress. We do have a big deadline approaching, and if we don't complete our work on time, production will have to stop until we do. This morning the copy machine broke down, which didn't help the situation. But Mr. Bell remained calm and kept to business as usual, right down to his three cups of coffee with lots of creamer. He even dipped his tie in his coffee cup like always. He was kind of clumsy that way."

Radley thought their escort might tear up at the memory, but North just shrugged and continued.

"All of his employees were on track with their annual goals and performance reviews, so there shouldn't have been any problems," she finished, as if that were the end of the topic.

"Thank you, Miss North," Radley said. "We'll let you know if we need anything."

"Oh, I'm afraid I can't leave you unescorted," North said. "Corporate policy."

"Understood," Radley said with a tight smile. She looked at Burton, who had a grin of his own. They started walking toward the bathroom.

"This reminds me of the Halloway case," Burton said, pulling a name out of the air. "Do you remember that one?"

"How could I forget?" Radley said, ducking her head to stifle a chuckle. North was one step behind them, well within earshot.

134

"The way his head kept oozing that stuff," Burton said, and looked around at North. "It's amazing what happens when a mucous membrane is stimulated with electricity. That was a lot of snot, let me tell you. Almost five gallons." North nodded, swallowed, and slowed her pace enough to let Burton and Radley get about ten feet in front of her.

"Snot?" Radley asked under her breath.

"It's the first thing I thought of," Burton murmured as they turned the corner to the bathroom. On the right was the open doorway to the copy room, and Burton saw a technician working on the bulky machine. He and Radley made a detour into the copy room, North right behind them.

"Hello, I'm Wes Burton with the crime lab, and this is Detective Radley."

"I didn't do it," the repairman said.

"You didn't do what?" Burton asked.

"Whatever happened."

"Do you know what happened this morning?" asked Radley.

"Look, guys," the repairman said, turning around. "I'm working on this as fast as I can, and I got people coming in here every five minutes to see if it's ready yet. I even skipped my morning break to keep working, so no, I don't know what happened, but I do know I didn't do it, because I've been in here all day. And once I do get it working, I still have this mess to clean up." He gestured at the table next to the copier, where several toner cartridges sat surrounded by powder that had leaked from them. At the back of the table were a coffee machine and various creamers and sugar replacements, along with a stack of foam cups and thin red stirrers.

"How long have these cartridges been here?" Burton asked.

"I pulled them out first thing," the repairman said, his head back in the machine.

"Can I have some coffee?" Burton asked North, who nodded. He leaned over the table and plucked a cup off the stack, then leaned farther to grab the pot and pour the hot coffee. To reach the creamer, he practically had to bend at a 90-degree angle.

"You're under arrest for murder," Burton told the cup of coffee and took a sip.

How did Bell get poisoned?

Burton's File

Bell had three cups of coffee that morning, with creamer. When I got a cup for myself, I had to bend over the table to reach everything. The table was covered in toner powder, which contains antimony, an element that causes symptoms similar to arsenic poisoning. Bell leaned over the table and dragged his tie through the powder, then accidentally dipped his tie in his coffee. Bell poisoned himself and didn't even realize it.

The Crime Is a Matter of Time

"This is an odd one," Burton said, and held up a file. Mike Trellis and Dr. Crown were in the crime lab examining a body. They both looked up.

"More odd than this guy?" Trellis asked. "He jumped out of a moving car at sixty miles an hour, fell into a ditch, and somehow managed to catch himself on fire. Twice."

"Maybe not as odd as that," Burton said. "But this is still a bit different than normal. Paula Larson, 42, just confessed to the January eighteenth murder of her fiancé, Denny Washington. She gave us the how and the why — she shot him with his own shotgun because he was stealing from her and was going to break up with her just before the wedding."

"So why are we involved?" said Trellis. "Sounds like everything is taken care of."

"Not quite," Burton said. "She claims it was a crime of passion, that she didn't plan to kill him. We have to prove her right or wrong. If it was premeditated, that makes it first-degree murder. If not, she might only get charged with voluntary manslaughter."

Trellis looked at Dr. Crown. "Do you take offense to that? The fact that it's always 'manslaughter,' whether the people involved were male or female?"

"No," Crown said.

"Do you take offense to anything?" asked Trellis. Crown

extracted the heart from the corpse and held it for a moment, pondering the question.

"I don't appreciate being referred to as a coroner," she said. "I'm a forensic pathologist." Burton and Trellis both saw that she was unconsciously squeezing the heart while she thought about being called a coroner.

Trellis looked at Burton nervously. "Let's leave the forensic pathologist to her work, shall we?"

"Good idea," Burton said. The two of them went to the other side of the lab, where they surveyed the evidence in the Paula Larson case.

"Larson panicked after she shot Washington," Burton said, pointing to a set of bloodstained bedsheets in sealed plastic bags. "Her statement says she pulled the bottom sheet off her bed, wrapped his body in it, and put the whole bundle into the trunk of her car. She drove around looking for a place to hide the body, but guilt overcame her and she drove to the police department instead."

"I wish all killers would be that courteous," Trellis said. "Tell her next time, she should bring a pizza, too."

"I'll pass it along," Burton said. "We also have the shotgun, the shell recovered from the scene, and the clothes both of them wore at the time of the shooting."

"I'll take a look at the clothes," Trellis said. "Just to make sure the gunshot residue and blood spatter match up with what she says happened."

"Don't assume anything she says is true," Burton said. "We need to learn for ourselves which shoes fit this evidence.

138

I'll examine the sheet; you let me know if you find anything."

They got to work, with Trellis laying out the clothes and checking bloodstain patterns. Burton did the same with the sheet, peering closely at the side of the fabric that had come in contact with Washington's body.

"I've got some fibers here," Burton said, plucking the fuzzy brown strands off the sheet with a pair of tweezers. "They look like paper, but I'll have to check them out under the microscope. Did you find anything yet?"

"Nothing to help or hurt Larson's case," Trellis said. "I did find a grocery receipt in her pants pocket dated January seventeenth, the day before the shooting. But it only has stuff on it like eggs, milk, bread, cereal, and so on. If she had purchased a copy of *How to Kill Your Fiancé and Get Away with It*, we might have something."

Burton was too busy looking into the microscope to respond. "These fibers are brown paper," he said. "Is there anything on Washington's clothes that could have transferred these fibers to the sheet?"

"No," Trellis said. "I found some lint and fuzz, but no brown-paper fibers."

"Hold on a minute," Burton said, and went back to the sheet. He examined the photos he had taken before touching anything in the trunk and spread the sheet out in the exact same way. Then he stood where Larson would have been when she put Washington's body into the car. "Washington was wrapped in the sheet like a burrito," he said, and mimicked lifting the body onto the sheet, then covering it as Larson had. "She pulled the top part of the sheet over him first, then covered that with the bottom part. So only the top flap actually contacted Washington's body. I recovered the fibers from the bottom flap, so they couldn't have come from him. They were already on the sheet when his body entered the trunk." Burton looked intently at Trellis. "I want you to go down to the interview room and ask Larson one question."

"Did you plan to kill your fiancé?" Trellis tried.

"No," Burton said. "Paper or plastic?"

How will the answer affect Larson's case?

Burton's File

The brown-paper fibers found on the sheet are from a grocery bag. Their presence on the fabric indicates that the sheet was in Larson's trunk on January 17, a day before the murder. Larson put the sheet there knowing she was going to kill Washington eventually, but in the meantime, she continued to place the usual things, such as groceries, in her trunk. Trellis referred to the whole situation as a "Gross series of events. Get it? Gross series . . . groceries."

The Evidence Will Float

Gibson poked at a stack of boxes on the workbench, and they almost toppled over.

"What's in these?" he asked.

"I haven't checked yet," Burton answered. "And if you knock them over, they'll be tainted evidence and inadmissible in court." The two of them were in Ron Carney's garage workshop, but Carney wasn't with them. He was in the interview room downtown with Radley, waiting for his lawyer to show up before he said anything.

"So do you think this guy is our thief?" Gibson said, clearly bored with the process of gathering evidence. Burton sighed, knowing that Gibson would continue to ask questions and make worthless remarks to pass the time.

"He fits the profile we're looking for," he responded, happy at least to be talking about the case rather than cars, Gibson's favorite topic. "He lives alone, has experience with tools and working with his hands, and has a few expensive items in his house that don't seem affordable for someone on his salary."

"Ever hear of credit cards?" Gibson asked.

"He doesn't have any," Burton said. "Which shows another trait we're looking for: a mistrust of the financial system."

"So how does he get into the places he robs?" Gibson said, flicking a light switch on and off.

"Don't do that, please," Burton said. "One of the reasons we're here is to see if we can find out how he gains access to the buildings without breaking in. Keep your eye open for keys, access cards, fake uniforms . . ."

"What if he crawled in through the air ducts?" said Gibson.

"Air ducts are designed to hold air, not men," Burton said. "He'd crash through the ceiling before he crawled ten feet. I'd like to think we didn't overlook something like that." Burton photographed a large piece of cardboard with bricks at the four corners, then moved all of that aside. Beneath was a four-foot-square table, the top covered with a flat piece of tin. He took a picture of that as well, then moved on.

"I see a small vacuum over here," Gibson said. "Should I at least clean up while I'm here? I feel kind of useless just standing around."

"You're not satisfied with your role of blocking my light and introducing offending odors into the crime scene?" Burton asked.

"I finished that job in the first fifteen minutes," Gibson retorted. "Do you want to see what's in the vacuum or not?"

"I'm giddy with excitement," Burton said, and took a photo of the small Shop-Vac. "Okay, open it up. Slowly, please." Gibson did so, and Burton saw the glitter of glass pieces in the vacuum's filter and tank. He took a few evidence bags out of vest pocket 9 and slipped a sample of the glass into each one.

"I think I might know how he's getting in and out without leaving a trace," Burton said. "At least, not one we can see with the naked eye. Let's go to the last robbery location and see if I'm right."

At Main Street Party Supply, the most recent business on the serial thief's hit list, Burton and Gibson stood outside the storefront and looked at the windows. It was 10 o'clock at night, and the shop was dark.

"See anything special?" Burton asked.

"Only you," Gibson said, then shook his head. "I don't see anything here. I don't even know what I'm looking for."

Burton reached into vest pocket 25 and pulled out his handheld ultraviolet light. He snapped it on and waved it along the windows until he reached the one closest to the door. The glass fluoresced under the black light, glowing a soft green. Burton turned off the light and measured the window.

"Four feet by four feet," he said. "Let's get back to the station. Whatever alibi Carney has, it's going to be as transparent as this piece of glass."

How did Burton know?

Burton's File

Carney scouted his targets and measured their windows before breaking in. He took those measurements home and made a window the exact same size as the one he intended to break, using a technique that involved pouring hot molten glass over liquid tin. When the "float glass" cools, it has small amounts of the tin on one side, which causes it to fluoresce, or glow, under black light. The four-foot-square tin table in Carney's workshop matched the four-foot-square window at Main Street Party Supply.

The Frozen Fisherman

Burton sat across from the suspect, Wally Potts, who was currently blowing his nose into a tissue. Gibson slouched in the corner behind Potts, his arms folded. He called this arrangement "The Hammer and the Anvil," because Burton laid the base of evidence out for the suspect, and Gibson smashed them against it with good old interrogation.

"Mr. Potts," Burton said. "This is what we know, just so we don't waste each other's time. You and Grant were the only ones in the ice fishing shack. The bruising on Grant's neck indicates he was suffocated from behind in a choke hold. Grant was found in the shack two days later by a park ranger, his body frozen stiff." Burton hoped this wealth of information would stun Potts into a confession.

"Stiff, that's funny," Potts said, sniffing. "Is that where the term comes from? Stiff, because the body is frozen?"

"No, it comes from rigor mortis," Burton said, "the chemical process that takes place in the muscles after death. The chemicals contract the muscles to make them rigid, locking the body in position. There are plenty of factors, but generally speaking, if the temperature is around seventy degrees Fahrenheit, the body will go from limp to completely stiff and back to limp again within forty-eight hours. But Grant's body hasn't gone through that process yet, because it was frozen soon after death. Now tell us what happened."

"Yeah," Gibson said. "Before he gets out his slide

projector and starts lecturing about trace fibers and blood spatters."

"That isn't until after lunch," Burton said. "Mr. Potts? We're waiting."

"Here's the deal," Potts said. "Grant and I went ice fishing on Sunday at his shack on the lake. I left before Grant did, and the last I saw of him, he was still sitting with his line in the water. That's all I know, and I'm not saying anything else." Potts coughed, covering his mouth with the crook of his elbow.

"Don't get me sick," Gibson said. "You think I'm ornery now, you ought to see me with the flu."

Burton shuddered at the thought. "How long have you had this cold?" he asked Potts. Potts considered the question for a moment to see if it was a trick.

"I came down with it on Friday," he said after deciding his sniffles couldn't incriminate him. Again, he coughed into the bend of his elbow.

"The contagious phase is two to four days," Burton told Gibson. "It's Wednesday, so we should be in the clear."

"Does that mean I can get in his face?" Gibson asked, a grin spreading across his own.

"You can do whatever you want," Burton said. "I'm going to take Mr. Potts's shirt to the lab and prove he killed Grant."

How will Burton do it?

Burton's File

Mr. Potts was sick since Friday, which means he was coughing in the ice shack on Sunday. He showed a habit of using the crook of his elbow to stifle his coughs, leaving plenty of DNA on his sleeve. Grant was suffocated from behind using a choke hold, which places the crook of the elbow's attacker against the victim's throat. A swab of Grant's neck, which had been frozen and preserved since the murder, showed a match to Potts's DNA, proving that Potts killed Grant. Gibson did end up with a cold, but it was due to his tendency to not wash his hands as often as he should.

The Guilty First Impression

"We need some impressions of those shoeprints in the mud outside," Burton said. He was standing in a huge barn next to the body of Kendall Luthey, who had been killed within the last 24 hours.

"Okay," Mike Trellis said. He found a clean spot on the floor and lay down. Detective Gibson walked in, looked at Trellis, and stopped.

"What are you doing?" he asked.

"This is my impression of a shoeprint," Trellis said. "Get it? Because I'm on the ground."

Gibson looked at Burton. "Can I shoot him?" he asked, pointing at Trellis.

"I'd rather you didn't," Burton said. "He still owes me for lunch yesterday. And he's going to have to skip lunch today if he doesn't get moving." Trellis scampered off to get the impression kit from the truck.

"Any leads yet on who may have been here with Luthey?" Burton asked as he snapped photos of the body. He noticed that Luthey's hands were very clean, with manicured nails. If there was any trace evidence under those nicely trimmed nails, it would be easy to spot.

"We ran the phone records," Gibson said. "One number was on there six times in the last day, and it belongs to a Mr. Evan Akers, who I just spoke with. He's on his way over right now. He says he was here last night, but when he left,

Luthey was alive and well. Apparently, they were working on some new engine design that they're going to patent." Gibson pointed toward a worktable covered with a tarp. "That's probably the engine. Want to have a look?"

"Not unless it becomes part of the investigation," Burton said. "Why is Akers coming here? He can't access the scene until we're done."

"He probably wants to make sure we don't steal his precious engine design. To be honest, I don't see how they could make one better than the Chevy Big Block V8," Gibson said.

"I don't even know what that means," Burton said, and headed out to see how Trellis was doing.

The mud had retained the shoeprints well, and Trellis had set up an angled light next to the prints to bring out their depth and detail. He was finishing up with the photography when Burton and Gibson joined him.

"These are good plastic prints," Burton said.

"Plastic?" said Gibson. "How can you tell the shoes were plastic? Like clown shoes?" Trellis almost dropped the impression kit he was carrying. He despised clowns.

"No," Burton said. "There are three basic types of shoeprints: patent, latent, and plastic. Patent means they're visible, like when someone walks through wet paint. Latent means they're invisible to the naked eye. Those happen, for example, when someone walks across a concrete floor and leaves traces from the soles of their shoes. Plastic prints, like these here, occur when you walk through soft materials like mud, snow, or sand and leave a three-dimensional print behind."

Trellis set a wooden frame around one of the shoeprints and was about to pour dental stone plaster in when Burton interrupted.

"You might want to spray it first, Mike," he said. Trellis nodded in agreement, then sprayed the shoeprint with clear shellac to harden the mud. Burton looked at Gibson, who seemed confused. "It helps keep the print from being distorted by the weight of the plaster," he told the detective.

"I know," Gibson said, quite unconvincingly.

"Right," said Burton. "Then you probably noticed that these particular prints have a distinct angle to them. The toe end of the shoe is much deeper than the heel."

"Of course," Gibson said. A large pickup truck pulled up in front of the barn. A skinny man with a greasy baseball hat jumped down from the driver's seat and strode toward them.

"That's close enough, Mr. Akers," Gibson said. "This is still a crime scene."

"Did you look under that tarp?" Akers demanded, pointing an oil-stained finger at them.

"What tarp?" Gibson answered. Burton was slightly amused — Gibson's approach to conversation was fun to listen to, unless he was talking to you.

"That engine is worth a lot of money," Akers said. "If you try to steal my idea, there's going to be trouble."

"Did Luthey try to steal your idea?" asked Gibson. Akers started to talk then caught himself.

150

"We were business partners," he said. "Fifty-fifty, that was the deal."

"Now, let's see," Gibson said. "I was never good at math, more of a wood-shop guy. But fifty percent plus fifty percent . . . that means you now get one hundred percent, right?"

"When I left here last night," Akers said, pointing that oily finger at the ground, "he was alive."

"Are these your shoeprints, Mr. Akers?" Burton asked, indicating the series of indentations that led from the barn. Akers had left a fresh set of tracks from his truck when he approached them, and Burton could tell they were the same, though not nearly as deep in the toe end as the older prints.

Akers looked at the prints, then his shoes. "I guess they are," he said.

"And when you left last night, Luthey was fine? You weren't in any hurry to leave?" asked Burton.

"That's right."

"Then why were you running away from the barn?"

How did Burton know?

Burton's File

Last night's shoeprints were deeper in the toe than they were in the heel, indicating that Akers had most of his weight on the front of his feet, as humans do when they run. The tracks he left from the truck when he showed up at the crime scene were

151

flat, and demonstrated what type of prints he left when he walked.

Akers's oily hands indicated that he did most of the work, while Luthey's clean hands and manicured fingernails suggested that he did not help much when it came to the labor. Akers felt that if they didn't split the work 50-50, they shouldn't split the money 50-50. In the argument that followed, Akers killed Luthey.

The Life-Saving Stomach

"Stop pacing, you're making me antsy," Detective Radley said.

"Sorry," Burton grumbled. "I don't like hospitals. They smell like sickness."

"So you prefer the smell of death over illness? That's pretty morbid," said Radley. "Do you know why you feel that way?"

Burton frowned at this for a moment, started to answer, then stopped. "Wait a minute," he said. "Are you asking out of concern, or are you looking for content for your book?"

"Both," Radley admitted. "I'm starting to figure out that criminals might not be as interesting as those who catch them."

Before Burton could comment on this, Dr. Felson emerged from the room in front of them.

"He's awake, but weak," Felson said. "If you need to speak with him, please make it short."

"Thank you, Doctor," Radley said as she opened the door. Burton followed, his hands in his pockets. He knew it was ridiculous, but he was wary of touching anything.

"Hello Mr. Kuhn, I'm Detective Radley. This is Wes Burton, he's a criminalist with our CSI lab. We'd like to ask you a few questions, if you're up for it."

"Sure, sure," Kuhn said. "Did I do something wrong?"

"Well," Burton said. "You didn't die."

"Beg pardon?" Kuhn said, leaning forward in his bed.

"We believe you were poisoned," Radley said, stepping in front of Burton and his poor bedside manner. "Someone gave you a lethal dose of cyanide, and we'd like to find out who."

"And how you survived the dosage," Burton added over her shoulder.

"Okay," Kuhn said. "Where do we start?"

Radley took out her notepad. "How about a list of everything you had to eat or drink in the last few days?"

"Wow, let's see," Kuhn started. "Today's Thursday, so on Monday, I had, let's see . . . grits and toast for breakfast, with OJ . . ." Kuhn continued with his list, compiling items that Burton would expect to see on a billy goat's menu. "Tuesday night I had tuna fish and broccoli, with pink lemonade to drink. Then on Wednesday, I had . . . wait, I didn't eat anything yesterday. Except those cookies. I can't resist a good cookie. Especially when they have almonds in them."

"Why didn't you eat anything else?" Radley asked.

"I ran out of my medication," Kuhn said. "I have to take betaine hydrochloride as a supplement. I have a stomach-acid deficiency, and without my meds, I can't really digest anything."

Burton looked at the chart at the foot of Kuhn's bed. "Hypochlorhydria," he read. "Your stomach doesn't produce enough hydrochloric acid."

"Yeah, that's right." Kuhn said. "How long do you think I'll have to stay here? I'm afraid if I'm gone too long, my landlady will throw my stuff in the street and rent my apartment to someone else."

"Did you and your landlady have an argument?" Radley asked, her pen poised above the notepad.

"Nah," Kuhn said, waving his hand. "It's in the lease that she can't raise my rent, so she's always teasing me about moving out so she can get a new tenant at a higher rate. But she doesn't really want me to leave. Heck, she baked me those cookies, so she must like me a little."

"You still might have to sign a new lease, though," Burton said. "After all, she won't be a very good landlady from prison."

How did Burton know she gave Kuhn the poison, and how did he survive?

Burton's File

Kuhn mentioned that he couldn't resist the almond cookies the landlady made for him. Cyanide has a distinctive bitter almond odor that the would-be killer covered up by adding almonds to the poisoned cookies. What the landlady didn't know was that Kuhn was off his medication and his stomach was not producing any hydrochloric acid, which is needed to start the chemical reaction that makes cyanide fatal.

The Missing Merrill

Burton met Dr. Crown in the lab's examination room and was surprised to find her in a very good mood.

"What are you so happy about?" he asked her.

"What makes you think I'm overly happy?" Crown asked back.

"You put an exclamation point on the note you left me," Burton said. "You wrote 'Meet me in the lab right away!' For you, that's like sending a parade and fleet of hot air balloons."

Crown looked at him a moment, seemingly upset that someone knew how she felt, then a small smile appeared. "Mrs. Merrill is here."

"Aha!" Burton said. "I should have known! You always get excited when we have to exhume a body."

"Well," Crown said. "We have the opportunity to possibly provide closure for those who are still grieving."

"And find a clue that someone else missed," Burton added.

"Yes, that, too," Crown said. "She's right over here." Crown and Burton walked to the farthest table in the exam room, where Mike Trellis was waiting with the body.

"Your first exhumed autopsy?" Burton asked him.

"Yup," Trellis said. "I figure this is as close as I'm going to get to examining a mummy."

"Michael," Crown said, "do you remember the talk we had about respect in the presence of the deceased?"

"Yes, Dr. Crown," Trellis said.

"Good. Now let's see what those inept jokers missed the first time around," said Crown.

"I read the file on this the other day," Burton said, securing his gloves and gown. "Mrs. Merrill died thirteen years ago, at age 57. She didn't receive an autopsy or even a wake before her funeral, and her husband asked for a closed-casket burial. Didn't any of that strike investigators as odd? Something they might want to look into?"

"At the time," Crown said, "Mr. Merrill was a powerful individual. He could have put pressure on certain people to make the whole thing go away as soon as possible." Crown opened the case file and pulled out a newspaper clipping that showed Mr. and Mrs. Merrill next to each other at the 1986 dedication of the downtown library. The tall man did strike an imposing figure, with Mrs. Merrill only coming up to his chest.

"Where is old man Merrill now?" Trellis asked.

"I believe he's at the courthouse as we speak, trying to stop us from pulling this sheet back," Crown said as she pulled the sheet back.

Something caught Burton's eye.

"Mike, do you have the X-rays that the lab took of Mrs. Merrill this morning?" he asked.

"They're in the file," Trellis said. Burton flipped through and found the X-rays, sorted those until he found the films of the humerus bones, and measured them.

"How tall is Mr. Merrill?" Burton asked the room.

"I've stood next to him," Crown said. "I'd put him at six-foot-two, give or take an inch."

"That's 74 inches," Burton muttered to himself. "In the photo, Mrs. Merrill comes up to his chest, which looks to be about three quarters of his height. So we'll put her at . . ."

"Fifty-five and a half inches," Trellis said.

Burton looked at the X-ray again. "Dr. Crown, will you please measure the upper arm bones on the body?"

Crown did, and reported her findings. "Right humerus is 13.25 inches, left humerus is 13 inches," she said.

"Call down to the courthouse and have Mr. Merrill detained," Burton said. "We need to ask him where his wife is. This isn't Mrs. Merrill."

How did he know?

Burton's File

A person's height is usually five times the length of their humerus (upper arm) bone. If Mrs. Merrill was only 55.5 inches tall, or approximately 4'6", her humerus would be 11 inches long instead of 13. Desiccation occurs as the body decomposes, which means the bones dry out and shrink. Even after this happened, the body in Mrs. Merrill's casket was at least a foot too tall.

The Pencil Points

Burton and Detective Gibson walked toward the small, cozy house on Cedar Street and saw a gray-haired man peek at them through the drapes, then duck back quickly.

"We've been spotted," Gibson said.

"Should we call for backup?" Burton asked.

"I don't think we need the SWAT team to handle Mr. Tanner," said Gibson, glancing down at Burton. "Besides, if he attacks, he'll go for the weaker-looking one of us first."

"I'll try to save you," Burton said, leaving Gibson with a scowl on his face. He knocked on the front door. The same gray-haired man peered through the curtained window in the door, and Burton could hear the sound of several locks being undone. The door inched open, and the man pressed his face into the crack.

"Yeah?" he said.

"Are you Ralph Tanner?" Burton asked.

"What's it to ya?" the old man said. Gibson stepped next to Burton on the front steps, and the old man gave him a distrusting glare.

"I'm Detective Gibson; pleased to meet you," Gibson said. "This guy here, you can call him Burton. He's from the crime lab."

Burton said, "Mr. Tanner, we just left the hospital where your wife has been admitted for emergency care. She had stomach pain and fits of vomiting — and she said that she thought you might be trying to kill her."

"If I was trying, she'd be dead!" Tanner spat and slammed the door shut.

"Nice work, Burton," Gibson said. "Now he's probably inside destroying evidence and our careers."

"Your career was ruined anyway," Burton said. He eyed the two garbage cans along the curb in front of Tanner's house. "Doesn't the area between the sidewalk and the road belong to the city?" he asked.

"Yeah, why?" Gibson said.

"Because maybe the evidence we're looking for isn't inside anymore," said Burton as he snapped on a pair of latex gloves from vest pocket 5. He handed a pair to Gibson, who took them like they were radioactive.

"This isn't part of my job description," Gibson said.

"Come on," said Burton. "Maybe you'll find a shirt you like. Or something for lunch." They lifted the lids off the garbage cans and were greeted immediately by the stench of warm filth.

"Reminds me of your aftershave," Burton said as he started sifting through the trash.

"Gacch, this is horrible!" Gibson said. "What are we looking for, anyway?"

"Mrs. Tanner said her husband kept telling her she needed more tea," Burton said, lifting a cluster of old tea bags out of the can. He placed them in an evidence bag from vest pocket 9. "She said it was kind of sludgy and tasted like it had

160

dirt in it, or clay. She said the more she drank, the sicker she felt. Finally, she drove herself to the hospital when Mr. Tanner refused to take her. He said she just needed more tea."

"How romantic," Gibson said. "Maybe he was using all these pencils to write her love letters." Gibson was steadily making a pile of broken pencils he found in the trash.

"That's a lot of pencils to throw away at one time," Burton said. Even though they were in pieces, he could tell there were at least twenty pencils so far.

"Well, no wonder they were tossed," Gibson said. "They're hollow." He squinted into the end of one of the segments, then passed it to Burton. The CSI looked at the piece, and sure enough, the center was empty.

"Get ready to kick that door in if you have to," Burton said. "These pencils just wrote Mr. Tanner's arrest warrant for attempted murder."

How did Burton know?

Burton's File

Mr. Tanner removed the cores of the pencils, crushed them into powder, and mixed it into Mrs. Tanner's tea, thinking it would give her lead poisoning. What he didn't know is that pencil lead actually contains no lead and never has; it's made from a mixture of graphite and clay. He only succeeded in giving her an upset stomach — and a husband in prison.

The Proof Is Hear

Dr. Crown looked up briefly when Burton entered the examination room, then went back to her microscope. She was expecting his visit but not the company he had with him.

"Dr. Crown, this is Gary Reardon," Burton said by way of introduction. "He's with the insurance company that covered Benny Owens." Burton gestured toward the body on the table, which was covered with a white sheet.

"Why are you here?" Crown asked Reardon. She didn't appreciate meddling in her lab, and tours were absolutely out of the question.

"Mr. Burton here says that you have proof that Mr. Owens did not jump to his death on purpose. That he fell," Reardon said. "Of course, my company doesn't cover suicide, so it's relevant to the surviving family and the company."

"Burton, is this true?" Crown asked, peering at him over her glasses. Burton seemed instantly uncomfortable. He knew it would bother Crown to have Reardon in her lab, but he was beginning to worry that she might kick them both out.

"Well, um," he started. "Mr. Reardon wasn't going to take my word for it, so I offered to show him the proof. And the proof's in here. So here we are." It sounded lame to his ears, and he could only imagine what Crown thought of his logic. She looked from him to Reardon and back again, then walked to the exam table.

"Let's get this over with," she muttered, much to Burton's relief.

"Okay, Mr. Reardon," Burton said as they approached the body. "Owens was setting up a four-story scaffold when he fell. That means he was working on the top of the tower as it was being built, so there were no rails or safety wires. He was wearing earplugs, eye protection, and a hard hat. He also should have been tied off, but that's not relevant. Shoulda woulda coulda."

"We've been over all of this," Reardon said. "We know he was in dangerous working conditions, but so was everyone else, and they didn't fall. Owens had a history of depression, and he and his wife weren't getting along very well at the time of his death. Nothing that I've seen indicates his fall was accidental."

"Then take a look at this," Burton said, and pulled the sheet away from Owens's head. He was hoping Reardon would cringe, look away, or at least lose the smug smile he had on his face. Instead, he leaned toward the body and shook his head.

"What am I looking for?" Reardon said, his tone suggesting he was a bit bored.

"You're looking for his hearing," Burton said, and handed him an otoscope with the light on. Reardon held the cone outside of Owens's left ear, peered through the lens, and stood up.

"I see an ear," Reardon said, with a roll of his eyes. "This is groundbreaking." Crown took the otoscope from him and inserted the cone almost all the way into Owens's ear.

"Look again," she said. Reardon did, and when he stood up this time, he was frowning. Burton smiled.

"I'm not a doctor," Reardon said. "But it doesn't look good in there."

"Otitis media," Burton said. "Or inflammation of the middle ear, if you prefer. The initial postmortem exam didn't catch it because he was such a mess from the fall. But after a thorough cleaning, Dr. Crown saw the infection."

Reardon considered this for a moment, then looked at Crown. "Nice work, Doctor. I'll pass the news on to the company. We'll deem Mr. Owens's death accidental."

What convinced Reardon?

Burton's File

At the time of his death, Owens had a serious middle ear infection and was wearing earplugs, which made the problem worse. If the outer and middle ear are healthy, they contain the same amount of atmospheric pressure (when you yawn and hear a pop, that's your middle ear equalizing the pressure). If the middle ear is infected, it cannot equalize the pressure and cannot transmit signals to the inner ear. The inner ear is very important when it comes to maintaining balance, something Owens needed to keep him from falling.

The Shattered Lie

"Good fences make good neighbors," Burton said while he snapped photos of Kevin Mahoney's living room. Glass from the shattered picture window covered the carpet, and a large brick sat in the middle of the broken shards.

"These guys would need a pretty big fence," Detective Radley said. "I'm talking Berlin Wall big."

"I was thinking the Great Wall of China," Burton said. "Let's see if we have this right. Mahoney says that he was watching TV when he saw his neighbor, Cliff Adams, in his front yard. Mahoney starts yelling at him through the window to get out of his yard, and Adams picks up this brick and chucks it through the window, yelling that he's going to kill Mahoney. So Mahoney grabs the .22 rifle he keeps above the fireplace and shoots Adams in the leg."

"That's what Mahoney says," said Radley. "According to Adams, he was walking through Mahoney's front yard — which he admits Mahoney doesn't like — when Mahoney starts yelling at him through the picture window. Adams ignores him and keeps walking, and Mahoney shoots at him through the window, striking him in the leg. Adams goes down, but manages to pick up this brick and throw it at Mahoney to try to keep him from firing again."

"So it's a case of he-said-he-said," Burton remarked. "Who do you believe?"

"I think they're both full of it," Radley said. "We have

records of police responding to multiple calls because these two can't live next door to each other without breaking into civil war every now and then. But one of them is flat-out lying."

Burton finished with his camera and took an evidence bag out of vest pocket 9. He slipped a few samples of the glass into the bag and sealed it. "Let's take a closer look at this brick," he said, taking a brush out of vest pocket 16 and fingerprint powder out of pocket 22. "Before I start, do you see anything special about this brick?" he asked Radley. She leaned in for a closer look. The brick was the standard size, shape, and color, with nothing on the surface but a little dirt from the front yard. Radley shook her head.

"Looks like a plain old brick to me," she said.

Burton nodded and began to dust for prints. When he was finished, there were three good fingerprints, one that was a bit smeared and one good thumbprint. "The thrower was left-handed," Burton said. "Is Adams a southpaw?"

"He is," Radley said, "and there was dirt on his left hand. We also have gunshot residue on Mahoney's right hand, so we know he's right-handed."

Burton picked up the brick and bagged it, careful to leave the bits of glass that were underneath it in place.

"So we know that Mahoney did shoot the gun," Radley continued, "and that Adams did throw the brick, but in what order? It's Adams's word against Mahoney's."

"No," Burton said. "It's Mahoney's word against the truth. He's the one who's lying."

How did Burton know?

166

Burton's File

Mahoney claimed he shot at Adams after his neighbor threw the brick through the window. However, the brick had no glass on top of it but did have pieces of glass beneath it, indicating that the window was already broken when the brick landed on the floor.

The glass in the living room also implicates Mahoney as the one who acted first. Regular glass is classified as a fluid and flexes like a trampoline when a bullet hits it. When the glass snapped back from the bullet's impact, the window shattered and the pieces sprayed into the living room.

The Story That Didn't Smell Right

Burton and Mike Trellis followed Ed, the border collie, around Charlie's Auto Repair Shop once more, then stopped for a rest. They had been trying to find the shop's owner for three hours, and Ed hadn't found any trails yet. If she had found something, she would have let Burton know by staring at the discovery and remaining perfectly still.

"Still no Charlie?" Trellis asked the dog. Ed looked at him, ears on full alert. Her nose tested the soft breeze that crossed the parking lot, but she didn't find any hint of Charlie in the air.

Trellis said, "What if he isn't missing, boss? What if he left on purpose?"

"That is possible," Burton said. He poured Ed a bowl of cool water set in the shade, and told her to take a break. "His wife reported him as missing, but he could have kept her in the dark about any plans he had to leave. Detective Radley is looking into the repair shop's accounting. Maybe that will shed some light on the situation."

"So the guy leaves for work yesterday morning," Trellis said, going over the details. "He doesn't come home that night, so his wife calls the police. According to the people who had appointments yesterday, the shop wasn't open. There was a note on the door that said CLOSED UNTIL

168

FURTHER NOTICE. SORRY! So he could have been missing since he left his house, right?"

"Right," said Burton. "And no one's been able to locate the repair shop assistant, Ben Page. So either he's in on Charlie's plan, or Charlie got rid of him to keep the plan secret." Burton's cell phone chirped, and he took it out of vest pocket 18. He looked at the display and saw that the caller was Radley.

"Hello?" he said in a high, raspy voice.

"Who is this?" Radley said, sounding confused.

"This is Ed," Burton said. Ed picked her head up at the mention of her name and swished her tail. Trellis put his finger to his lips and motioned for Ed to be quiet, so as not to ruin the trick.

"What? Who?" Radley said.

"Ed, the border collie," Burton said. "Wes can't come to the phone right now. He's busy being cool and laughing at Mike's jokes."

"Okay, now I know you're lying," Radley said.

"But you believed it was Ed until that point?" Burton asked, back to being Burton.

"Almost," said Radley. "But Ed has a Scottish accent. I thought you knew that."

"You're right," Burton said. "I guess that's why you're the detective. Did you find anything in the repair shop accounts?"

"Someone has been stealing money from the place," said

Radley. "The books don't add up. There's a difference of about fifty thousand dollars so far, and that's only the past year."

"Yikes," Burton said. "We were at Charlie's house earlier. He and his wife didn't have any extra yachts or sports cars lying around."

"Maybe he's hiding it until later," Radley said. "Or hiding it from his wife."

"Hey, boss," Trellis said, and nodded toward the driveway. Burton looked, and saw a truck pulling in. CHARLIE'S AUTO REPAIR SHOP was stenciled on the door.

"I'll call you back," Burton said into the phone, then switched to the Ed voice. "I will, too!"

"Can't wait," Radley said, and hung up.

Burton and Trellis met the truck as it eased to a stop in front of the shop. A man got out of the driver's seat, looked at them, and nodded.

"Did you find him yet?" he asked.

"Find who?" Burton said. "And who are you?"

"I'm Ben Page," he said. "I worked here with Charlie for three years. Then yesterday, out of the blue, he says he's leaving. He gives me this big hug, tells me thanks for all my work, and then he's gone." Page looked at the ground, not knowing what to say next.

"He didn't mention where he was going?" Burton asked.

"Not to me," Page said. "Man, we were best friends. That doesn't happen often in a boss-employee relationship, let me tell you. So, in the same day, I lost my job and my buddy."

"What have you been doing since then?" Trellis said.

"Driving around," Page said. "I waited in the shop for a few hours, and when he didn't come back, I just drove around. Ended up cruising all night." He looked down at his shop uniform and shook his head. "I haven't even changed my clothes or taken a shower."

Ed, who seemed to know when people needed cheering up, trotted over to Page and gave him a sniff, her tail wagging. She sat next to his feet and gazed up at him, obviously in need of some ear scratching.

"Well, hello there," Page said. "Is this your dog?"

"Yes, her name's Ed," Burton said. "And she just told me that your story is a lie."

What did Ed do?

Burton's File

It's more a question of what Ed didn't do. Page said that Charlie gave him a big hug when he left and that he hadn't had a chance to change his clothes yet. If that were true, Ed would have smelled Charlie on Page's clothes and stood perfectly still, staring at the mechanic. Instead, she sat and wagged her tail. Page has some explaining to do, thanks to the Ed Lie Detector.

The Toilet Tank Test

"You already know what happened, don't you?" Trellis said as soon as he saw Burton in the large bathroom. He just had that look on his face.

"I might," Burton said with a small smile. "Let's see if you can figure it out." Trellis frowned. He didn't mind Burton's surprise tests, but he knew he was on a tight schedule. Burton wouldn't let quiz time interfere with procedure.

"Can I get some more light in here?" Trellis asked. The bulb in the ceiling fixture above the toilet was missing, and the room was dimly lit by the hall light.

"If you need it," Burton said, not quite mocking but close. The frown on Trellis's face deepened, and he stepped into the bathroom.

"That is an extraordinary amount of blood," Trellis said.

"Amazing, isn't it?" Burton asked. "The human body only holds about six quarts, but spray just a pint of that on a wall and it looks like a massacre." He took one last photo, then set his camera down outside the doorway. The bathroom had enough spatter in it that setting anything down in the room could disturb evidence. There was blood on the tiled walls and floor, the sink, the toilet, and the body of Hank Roberts, who was slumped against the wall across from the toilet.

"Is all of that blood from the deceased?" Trellis asked.

"I think so, but the lab will find out for sure," Burton said.

"There does seem to be a difference in coloring," Trellis said. "We have dark red blood on Roberts's head and face, and the toilet tank lid over there," he said, pointing to the broken ceramic slab, which lay near the bowl, "with spatters of the same color going from the toilet to the body." He indicated the path with his finger, and Burton nodded at the maroon circles that led across the room.

"Then we have this bright red blood on the walls, floor, and Roberts's face and chest," Trellis continued, indicating the fine, elongated spatters. "But there's no blood on the ceiling or the wall opposite Roberts." Trellis mimicked holding the toilet tank lid and striking Roberts in the head with it several times. "If someone had killed him like this, blood would have gotten on the toilet tank lid, and when the killer swung the lid up, they would have sprayed cast-off blood all over the place, including the opposite wall and ceiling."

"Most likely," Burton said.

"Powder and brush, please," Trellis said, and Burton handed him the items from vest pockets 22 and 16, respectively. Trellis dusted the toilet tank lid but found nothing.

"So there aren't any fingerprints on the lid, and the blood on it shows that it hasn't been wiped." Trellis was starting to roll now, the sequence of possible events playing through his head quickly. "What injuries does Roberts have?" he asked.

"Preliminary examination shows a fractured skull and at least two broken ribs," Burton said. "X-rays will tell us if

173

there are any other broken bones, but those were pretty apparent. You can see where —"

"Don't tell me!" Trellis yelled. He knew that if Burton got going, he would forget all about the unofficial test and rattle off his conclusions before Trellis could reach his own. "The assailant wore gloves," he said, "and only hit Roberts once. That's why there isn't any castoff on the ceiling and wall."

"If he only hit him once," Burton said, "where did all of this other spatter come from?" He pointed to the bright red specks on the wall, floor, and Roberts. From their shape, Trellis could tell that the blood had hit the surfaces at a high speed.

"The attacker struck him with the tank lid once," Trellis said, knowing he was guessing, "then hit Roberts several times after that with his fists, or an object that he took with him."

Burton just pointed to the ceiling and opposite wall.

"I know, I know," Trellis said. "That would have caused castoff, too. Okay, you win. What happened here?"

"What happened is," Burton said, "you didn't check the entire scene before speculating about what happened. Look on the other side of the toilet."

Trellis had a moment of terror in which he imagined what he might find there. But when he did look, all he saw was a lightbulb. He picked it up with gloved fingers and put it over his head.

"Aha!" he said. "The conclusion has arrived!"

How did Roberts die?

Trellis's File

Burton got me this time. He was right, I didn't check the scene thoroughly. Roberts was standing on his toilet, trying to replace the lightbulb in the ceiling fixture and slipped. He hit his head on the toilet tank lid, breaking it and his skull. His chest hit the toilet bowl, fracturing his ribs and puncturing his lung. The dark red blood was from his head wound and it left a trail of drops to his body. The bright red blood was due to his punctured lung. Oxygen-rich blood is always bright red, and it dripped from his nose and mouth every time he exhaled. Roberts didn't have an attacker, unless someone has figured out how to sue a toilet.

The Tooth of the Matter

Burton saw the Sensitive Cleaners van parked at the curb and pulled in behind it. Bug was talking to a woman in the front yard, and she seemed to be taking a half step away from him every five seconds or so. Burton approached them, bracing himself for what Bug had to say. But he still was shocked when he got within earshot.

"So the possum poops, they are not so soft," Bug was saying to the woman, who took another step away from him. "So they are easier to clean up. Raccoons, everhow, they leave such messes. I don't like raccoons."

"Hello, Mr. Gorlach!" Burton called before the woman broke into a sprint.

"Ah, Burtons! You drive like syrup runs uphill!" Bug said by way of greeting. "We have been waiting for you for years!" He shook Burton's hand roughly then turned to the woman, who looked relieved to be done with her conversation. Or so she thought.

"This is Mrs. Krause," Bug said. "I am telling her about differences in animal droppings, since it is why she called me. She thought it was a squirrel who used her basement for a toilet, but it wasn't." Bug looked at Burton, waiting for the CSI to ask what kind of animal it was. This was all very exciting for Bug.

"So it wasn't a squirrel?" Burton asked. Bug shook his

head, a sly smile creeping onto his face. His lips moved silently, as if they could barely hold back the answer.

"What kind of animal was it?" Burton said.

"Rats!" Bug hollered. "Big ones, too! Not like rats from back home, though. Those rats tip over cars and eat tires. Mrs. Krause's rats, they come into her basement through crack in foundation, have party, and leave. Not so terrible."

"I hope you didn't call me here because the rats invited you to the afterparty," Burton said, "and you need a date."

"No, no! Come with me, I will show," Bug said.

"I'll stay out here," Mrs. Krause said. From the look she was giving her house, Burton wouldn't be surprised to find a moving truck in the driveway by the time he returned. He followed Bug through the front door and into the basement, where the rat feces were sitting along one wall.

"This is the biohazard," Bug said. "Rodents infest, and some could have the deadly hantavirus. We are safe, but don't kick dookie around or sniff it."

"I'll do my best," Burton said.

"This is why I call you, Burtons," Bug said, and pointed near the crack in the concrete foundation. "Do you see it?"

There was dirt spilling onto the basement floor from the crack, and Burton assumed some of the soil had come from the rats. He leaned a bit closer and finally did see it: a tooth.

"The tooth? Is that what I'm looking for?" Burton asked as he snapped on a pair of gloves from vest pocket 5.

"Yes, yes," said Bug. "Is it person?"

"Hard to tell right away," Burton said, and took a few photos of the small off-white bone. "A lot of animal bones can look very similar to human. A front bear paw looks a lot like a human hand, and a rib cage from a deer can easily be mistaken for a person's. But we won't know for sure until we run the DNA or find the rest of the skeleton." He plucked the tooth out of the dirt and brushed it off, carefully turning it in his hands. A glint of silver caught his eye. He nodded and slipped it into an evidence bag from vest pocket 9.

"You will have Ed sniff the ground to find the body?" Bug asked hopefully. Bug never tired of throwing the tennis ball for Ed, which made him one of her best friends.

"I don't have her with me today," Burton said as they made their way up the stairs. "But we can try a few other ways to find the burial spot." Outside the house, along the same wall as the foundation crack, Burton took a portable conductivity meter out of vest pocket 28.

"What is this?" Bug asked when he saw the tool.

"It tests how well the soil conducts electricity," Burton said. "The higher the number it reads, the more conductive the soil is."

"This dirt is electrifying?" Bug said, eyeing the ground.

"It doesn't contain electricity, but the moisture in the soil allows electricity to pass through," said Burton. "So if the soil has a lot of moisture, it will give a higher reading on the meter. You wait here, this shouldn't take long." He started at one corner and made his way along the wall, taking a measurement of the ground every four feet. The measurements came back 2.0, 2.15, 2.1, 4.6, 2.3, 2.0, and 2.2.

Burton walked back to the spot that measured 4.6 and began to run his CRIME SEEN? tape. "Congratulations, Bug. You helped find a buried human being."

How did he know the skeleton was human, and how did he know where it was buried?

Burton's File

The flash of silver in the tooth was a filling, and only a human tooth would have that. The 4.6 reading on the conductivity meter indicated that the soil in that spot contained more moisture than the others. When a buried body decomposes, it adds moisture to the surrounding soil.

The Walking Stiff

"He was a zombie, I tell you! A zombie!"

Burton could hear the man in the interview room yelling from across the hall, and he looked at Mike Trellis for an explanation. The CSI technician was dressed in his usual Halloween costume, which consisted of him carrying around a cereal box with a knife stuck in it. A new administrative assistant walked by, and Trellis said "I'm a cereal killer. Get it?"

The woman kept walking.

"She's upset because my costume is better than hers," Trellis said to Burton.

"Right," said Burton. "What's this I hear about a zombie?"

"Oh, that guy," Trellis said, frowning toward the interview room. "It's Jim Lee, the new part-time morgue attendant. He's freaking out because he thinks he saw a dead guy walking around."

"Well, it is Halloween," Burton said. "The day when the dead rise and walk the earth, and we have to dress like corpses to blend in with them."

"If that's the reason for Halloween, why are there so many clown costumes?" Trellis asked, his voice rising to a manic pitch.

"Because even the dead won't mess with clowns," Burton

said as they made their way toward the interview room. Inside, Detective Frank Gibson was standing and shaking his head at Jim Lee, who was sitting with his face in his hands.

"It was awful! Just awful!" Lee said. "Now I have to find a new job! I can't possibly stay in a work environment that has the undead walking around."

"I don't know," Gibson said. "Seems like it would be nice and quiet. Except for all that shuffling that zombies do."

"Mr. Lee," Burton said. "Can you take us through what happened? Hopefully, we can find a logical explanation for this incident."

"Incident?" Lee cried. "How about earthshaking event! The dead have returned!"

"Right, we've got that part," said Burton. "But take us through it, just the same." Lee took a deep breath, sipped his water with a shaky hand, and started talking.

"I was processing the paperwork for Warren Trudeau, who passed away last week. You probably remember him? You discovered evidence that he was murdered, but the killer hasn't been caught yet." Burton couldn't tell if that was a compliment or an insult, but he could see how Gibson took it by the detective's clenched jaw.

"I recall that case," Burton said. "There were signs of a struggle, but no trace of the assailant. There were two coffee cups on the table, and one of them had smudges that indicated fingerprints had been wiped off. But they both had Trudeau's DNA along the rim."

Gibson nodded. "We think the killer was looking for a winning lottery ticket Trudeau had. We found it hidden in his shoe during the autopsy. He must have told someone about it before he went to cash it in. We tried to contact his family to see if he told them, but the only person I've been able to track down is his brother — Dan, I think — and he hasn't called me back."

"Anyway," Lee said, "I put Trudeau in the cooler and filed his paperwork, then cleaned the area. About an hour later, I look up from my desk and see him walking around! I couldn't believe it! He was looking through drawers, opening cabinets, and when he finally got to my office, he looked in, saw me, and said 'Boo!' "

"The zombie said 'boo'?" Burton asked.

"I thought zombies just groaned," Gibson said. "You know: *uuuuuuuuhhhhh.*"

"No," said Trellis. "Zombies say 'brains.' They just walk around going 'Brains . . . brains . . .'" Gibson and Trellis did their zombie impressions, shuffling into the corners and flapping their arms while Burton and Lee watched.

"All right," Burton said when it was over. "That was charming."

"So," Lee said, glancing at all three of them. "Is there a plan for when zombies start to take over? Because I'm not really sure what to do."

"Yes, there is," said Burton. "We take fingerprints."

"That doesn't sound very helpful," Lee said.

"You said you cleaned before you saw the zombie," said

Burton. "So the zombie's fingerprints will be the only ones on the drawers and cabinets, right?"

"I guess," Lee said. "I did a pretty thorough job."

"Mike," Burton said to Trellis. "Head down to the morgue and lift some prints off those surfaces, then meet me in the lab."

"What should I do?" Gibson asked.

"You can go back to doing your zombie impersonation," Burton said. "Or was that how you do your thinking? I've never seen either, so I don't know."

Less than an hour later, Trellis and Burton met in the lab. "Here are the zombie's prints," Trellis said. Burton placed one of them under one side of the comparison microscope, and put Trudeau's print under the other. He peered into the eyepieces, then stepped back and let Trellis have a look.

"They don't match," Trellis said. "So who is the zombie?"

"I'll give you a hint," Burton said. "He was there when Trudeau died, and he was there when he was born."

Who was the zombie?

Burton's File

The zombie was Warren Trudeau's identical twin, Dan. Warren told his brother about the winning lottery ticket and Dan tried to get it from him but ended up killing his twin in the process. Dan went to the morgue to sort through Warren's belongings in the hope that the ticket was there.

Identical twins have the same genotype, or DNA; that's why all the DNA at the crime scene appeared to belong to Warren. But they do not share the same phenotype, which determines such physical traits as fingerprints.

The Wise Deduction

Burton approached the ditch along the country road and spotted Detective Frank Gibson standing in the weeds alongside the culvert. The burly detective waved him over, a large paper cup of coffee in his hand and a sly grin on his face. Despite the chilly weather, Gibson seemed to be in fine spirits.

"I don't like the looks of this at all," Burton muttered to himself. When he was within earshot, he found out why Gibson was so happy.

"Looks like they beat you to it," Gibson said, the smile spreading. He pointed to the yellow-and-black CRIME SCENE tape strung around an area of the ditch. "You won't be able to put up your cute 'crime seen?' tape today. What a shame."

Burton stopped next to the grinning detective. "I hope you didn't call me out here just for that," he said.

"No, no," Gibson reassured him, the smile gone. "Obviously we detectives and uniformed cops can't figure out what happened here, so we had to call the mighty Wes Burton to hold our hands." Gibson sniffed the cup of coffee he was holding. "Wait a minute! This smells like coffee! I think the killer drinks coffee!" He held the cup at arm's length and squinted at it. "Hold on, I think I brought this coffee with me. But I'm just a detective, so I can't tell for sure. Burton, will you check the cup for my fingerprints?"

While Burton waited patiently for Gibson to finish his rant, he checked his watch twice, popped a piece of gum in his mouth, and retied his shoe. When the detective was done jabbering, Burton gave him a flat look.

"What's the situation?" Burton asked.

Gibson took a sip of his coffee, smacked his lips a few times, and finally decided to let Burton in on the details.

"A farmer found a skeleton in the ditch. We think it might be Nate Robertson, that sixteen-year-old who went missing last year."

"And he's been here the whole time?" Burton asked. "This isn't exactly a highway, but I'm sure someone has been down this road in the past year."

"The farmer says this ditch has a few feet of water in it during the spring and most of the summer," Gibson said. "And with the sudden snow we had last fall, I'm not surprised no one spotted the body. I didn't take a real close look, but it looks like a gunshot to the head was the checkmate on this one."

Burton eased down the slope into the ditch, careful to keep some distance from the skeleton. If any bones had detached and relocated, he didn't want to disturb them. The skeleton was lying faceup, with the skull tilted a bit to the left. He was happy to see that the teeth were intact; maybe they could identify the body with dental records. For both the upper and lower sets of teeth, he counted four incisors, two canines, two pairs of premolars, and three pairs of molars, taking close-up photos the entire time. He looked at the hole in the skull just above where the right ear would have been, and shined his flashlight into it.

"I see the hole," he said to Gibson. "It does look like a bullet entrance, and I don't see an exit yet, so hopefully the slug is still in the skull."

"I also noticed some scratches and scrapes on the skull," Gibson said. "Looks like whoever it was took a beating, either before or after the shooting."

Burton shook his head. "Those are most likely post-mortem and not from the killer," he said. Gibson looked confused.

"Animals," Burton explained. "Most likely rats and coyotes. Their teeth and claws scratched the skull when they were trying to get their meal off of it." Gibson looked at his coffee and set it down, suddenly no longer interested in any type of food. Burton smiled.

"We can confirm with dental records," he said. "But I can tell you right now this isn't the body of Nate Robertson."

How did Burton know?

Burton's File

The skeleton's teeth included three pairs of molars on both the upper and lower sets. The third pair of molars, sometimes referred to as wisdom teeth, typically don't appear until the age of seventeen to twenty-five. The skeleton had fully developed wisdom teeth, indicating that it could not be sixteen-year-old Nate Robertson.

Too Much Billiards
on the Brain

Dr. Crown began to gently pull the top of Gary Wolfe's skull off, then stopped. Burton and Trellis were looking on with a mixture of anticipation and apprehension. Crown looked at them, then let go of the skull, leaving it in place for the time being.

"What is it?" Burton asked. Spatter a brain on a wall, and he could tell you where it came from, what put it there, and how fast it arrived. But leave it in the skull, and he was a bit lost.

"I want to give Michael a quick lesson in brain damage," Crown said.

"Isn't that kind of like giving a fish a lecture on being wet?" Burton asked.

"Ha-ha," Trellis said. "You want a real joke? Can I at least see the brain first, if you don't mind?" Trellis asked. "Get it . . . Brain . . . mind?" Crown shook her head.

"What would be the point if you don't know what you're looking for?" she said, already entering instructor mode. "When there is an injury to the head, two kinds of trauma typically occur: coup and countercoup. Coup takes place at the point of impact, or where the brain was struck. Counter-coup is directly opposite that point, on the other side of the head."

Crown picked up a container of waterless hand sanitizer,

the clear plastic showing the thick substance inside. "Think of this container as your skull, and the fluid inside as your brain. As you can see, when I strike the side of the skull with a moving object, the brain is damaged at the point of impact and pulls away from the skull." Crown karate-chopped the side of the container, and Burton and Trellis watched the contents fly away from the side of the strike.

"However," Crown said, "if the skull is the moving object, such as when someone falls and hits their head on the ground, the most trauma occurs opposite the impact point." She held the container upright, then swung it 90 degrees and slapped it into the palm of her hand, stopping the movement abruptly. The contents pulled away from the side opposite her hand, leaving a few bubbles behind. Trellis imagined his brain sloshing around in his head like that and shivered.

"All right, then," Crown said, squirting a bit of the sanitizer onto her hands. "Tell me what you know about the case."

Trellis immediately referred to his notes, eager to look away from Dr. Crown as she smeared the "brains" over her hands. "Our examination of the body showed cause of death to be a fracture at the back of the skull, with a blue powdery substance in the hair."

Crown nodded at this and motioned for Trellis to continue. "The witness report states that Wolfe was playing 9-ball billiards with some friends in his garage. He was sitting down and leaning back in his chair, and he tipped over backward and cracked his head on the floor. His friends tried to revive him and called 911, but he was pronounced dead before he reached the hospital." Trellis showed Crown some photos of the crime scene. They included a shot of the billiard table, with nine balls spread out across the green felt.

"Whoever shot first didn't do very well," he said. "They didn't get any balls in the pockets. That's all I have. Should we look at the brain now?"

"I think the time has come," Crown said. She stepped forward and eased the top of Wolfe's skull off, exposing the gray matter underneath. She gave a small nod, as if what she saw confirmed what she already suspected.

"There is substantial hemorrhaging around the occipital lobe," Crown said, indicating the rear of the brain. Trellis leaned in for a better look, a grimace on his face.

Burton did not look, because he was busy examining the photos of the billiard table. He counted nine balls, and the report stated that the group had indeed been playing 9-ball. The billiard balls were lying so that he could see at least a partial amount of the number on each.

"Hey, boss," Trellis said to Burton. "You want to take a look at this? We think maybe Wolfe didn't die from his head hitting the ground."

"I know he didn't," Burton said. "And I have a description of the killer. It's white, round, and missing from this billiard table."

How did Wolfe die?

Burton's File

Crown's explanation of coup versus countercoup indicates that Wolfe died from the impact of a moving object to the back of his skull. If he had hit his head on the ground like witnesses claimed, the internal bleeding would have been at the front of the brain, not the rear.

Wolfe and his friends were playing 9-ball, and there were nine balls on the table, but there should have been a tenth: the cue ball. The blue powder around Wolfe's fracture suggests cue chalk, which rubbed off of the cue stick, onto the ball, and onto Wolfe's head when the cue ball struck him.

The Stinky Ceiling Stain

Burton and Mike Trellis followed the vacuum hose from the Sensitive Cleaners van into the apartment building, up two flights of stairs, and through an open apartment door. Inside, Bug was standing with a man and a woman, all three of them looking up at the ceiling.

"What's up?" Trellis said. "Get it? Because you're looking up."

"Bah-ha-ha!" Bug laughed, bending over and holding on to the woman to keep from falling over. He laughed for almost a minute before he could speak. "Ah, Mikes, your words are like laughing gas, only not flammable."

"Thanks, Bug," Trellis said, and looked at Burton. "See? He thinks I'm funny."

"He also makes money cleaning up rat poop," Burton said. "I think his tastes might be a little unique." Burton turned to Bug. "What's the story here?"

"Ah, Burtons," Bug said. "I am called here by Stans and Katherines to clean up a stain on their ceiling. When I see it and then smell it, I know right away you should take looks before I do anything." Stan and Katherine looked confused, but they nodded anyway.

"Thanks for thinking of me," Burton said. He looked up at the stain on the ceiling. "Mostly brown, but I see some dark red here and there. And you're right, Bug, it smells bad.

Stan, Katherine, do you know who lives in the apartment above you?"

"That's Mr. Walton," Katherine said. "But we haven't seen him for a few days. You don't think he . . . died, do you?"

"Maybe we should go upstairs and see what Mr. Walton has to say about it," Burton said. "Mike, can you call the apartment manager and ask him to meet us upstairs with a key?"

"You got it," Trellis said, and started dialing.

"Is big mess," Bug said to no one in particular. "When body decays, it leaks all over floor. Sometimes bursts, you know, pop!"

Stan looked like he might faint, and Katherine started covering the furniture and carpet with trash bags in case the stain decided to spread.

"Bug," Burton said, "why don't you come upstairs with us?"

"Ah, yes, good," Bug said. "Stans, Katherines, do you want to come, too?"

Burton didn't think it was possible, but Stan and Katherine both got paler. They didn't know what to say.

"They'd better stay here," Burton said. "If it is a crime scene, we can't have any unauthorized personnel." Bug nodded, happy that he was authorized.

Burton, Trellis, and Bug went upstairs and met the apartment manager at Mr. Walton's door.

"Who has to pay for this if the guy died and left a mess?" the manager said.

"I'm sure your insurance will cover it," Burton said. "But we don't know that anyone died, so please open the door."

The manager unlocked the door and stepped back.

Mr. Walton's body was lying faceup in the middle of the living room. The smell inside was much worse, and Burton pulled three filter masks out of vest pocket 13. He handed one to Trellis and one to Bug, but Bug already had his own. It was better than the ones Burton had, with two filters instead of one. And it looked cooler, with black rubber and chrome fasteners.

"Do you have any more of those?" Trellis asked him.

"No, sorry," said Bug. His mask made him sound like a robot. Trellis shrugged and put on the mask Burton gave him, but he wasn't happy about it.

Burton figured out quickly why the room smelled so bad.

"That's a very large humidifier over there," he said, pointing to a large device against the wall that was still humming. "And the temperature has to be around eighty-five. With the high heat and humidity, Mr. Walton has been decaying at a very rapid rate. Bug, please stand here by the door while Mike and I check the body."

"But I am authorized," Bug said.

"Right," said Burton. "I need you to make sure no unauthorized people get in."

"Just let them try," Bug said, pulling a can of industrial cleaner out of his belt pouch. He stood in the doorway facing out, giving a suspicious look to the manager and everything else in the hallway.

194

"I wish we could bring him to every scene," Burton said. He and Trellis approached Mr. Walton's body, careful not to step in any of the fluids that had spread across the floor. The skin had started to change from dark purple to greenish-black, except for pale spots on the forehead, left cheek, and jaw. There was almost no blood beneath these spots.

"How long do you think he's been here?" Trellis said.

"Could be only a few days, with the climate in here," said Burton.

Trellis said, "Stan and Katherine are *not* going to be happy when they find out what that stain on their ceiling is."

"That's nothing," said Burton. "Wait until they discover that someone knew he was dead and didn't tell anyone."

How did Burton know?

Burton's File

When a body dies, the blood stops moving through the blood vessels. Gravity pulls the blood to the lowest areas of the body and creates a purplish discoloration called lividity. However, any part of the body that presses against a surface, such as the floor, remains pale because the weight of the body prevents the blood from settling there.

The pale spots on Mr. Walton's face indicate that he died facedown, and lividity set in while his face was pressed against the floor. Someone found him that way and rolled him onto his back but didn't inform the authorities.

Glossary

Abrasion — When skin is worn or rubbed away.

Accelerant — A flammable material used to start a fire.

Asphyxiate — To die from a lack of oxygen to the brain.

Autopsy — The examination of a corpse to determine or confirm h.

Blood spatter — The pattern of blood deposits at a crime scene that can help determine what occurred at the scene.

Compress — To press or squeeze.

Convict — **n.** A person found guilty of an offense or crime. **v.** To prove someone guilty of a crime in court.

Cranium — The skull.

Cyanoacrylate — Also known as superglue, it is fumed over substances to reveal fingerprints.

Deceased — A body that is no longer living.

Decompose — When a body starts to decay or break down after death.

DNA — The molecule that carries the genetic information in the cell. Traces of DNA from saliva, skin, blood, and other sources can be used to identify the person who left the trace.

EMT — Emergency medical technician.

Evidence — Any physical item that assists in proving or disproving a conclusion. For example, a paint scraping is evidence; an eyewitness account is not.

Gas chromatograph/mass spectrometer (GC/MS) — A system of instruments used to separate a complex mixture and identify its components.

Glucose — The main circulating sugar in the blood and the major energy source of the body.

GSR — Gunshot residue, the trace materials left behind when a gun is fired.

Hemorrhage — A rapid and sudden loss of blood.

Homicide — The killing of one person by another.

Hypoglycemia — An abnormally low level of glucose in the blood.

Laceration — A jagged wound or cut.

Lividity — The discoloration of the skin caused by the settling of blood that occurs in a body after the heart stops.

Marbled — Patterned with veins or streaks of color resembling marble.

Postmortem — Occurring after death.

Stippling — The deposit of unburned powder and other gunshot residue on a bullet wound. It can help determine the distance between the shooter and the victim.

Toxicology — The analysis of poisons and drugs in the blood and body fluids.

Trace element — A very small bit of chemicals or evidence.

Trajectory — The path of an object moving through the air.

UV light — Ultraviolet light, also known as black light, is used to identify many trace evidence items such as body fluids, drugs, and inks.

When the suspect's story is shaky, the evidence is solid!

CRIME FILES:

FOUR-MINUTE FORENSIC MYSTERIES

SHADOW OF DOUBT

by Jeremy Brown

CRIME SCENE - DO NOT C

SCENE - DO NOT CROSS

CRIME SCENE - DO

Break out your stopwatch and match wits with CSI Wes Burton and the best forensic team on the force to solve 50 brand-new mysteries!

◼ SCHOLASTIC

www.scholastic.com

CF2T